"Well. *That* certainly was refreshing."

Max climbed out from under the sink and shook the water from his hair. His cheeks gleamed with water and his shirt clung to his muscles.

Water dripped from the ceiling and appliances where the broken faucet had sprayed.

"You're all wet," Lacey said, her eyes taking in the clinging shirt, his impressive chest.

"You, too." Max drew his finger lightly across the front of her blouse. "Black lace. Nice," he murmured.

A little thrill went through her at the touch of his finger. They stared at each other in longing, the heat between them mounting, creating steam in the damp room.

"You tempt me too much." His hands cupped her face, his thumb gently brushing her lip.

He kissed her, long and sweet and hard. Just when her knees were about to buckle, he broke it off. "We can't do this, Lacey. It's not that simple."

"Don't think about it, Max," she whispered, teasing his mouth with her own. "Just give in."

Dear Reader,

Mmm, that cowboy thing. Sometimes we think the way a guy looks, dresses or moves tells us all we need to know about him. That's what happened with Lacey. Luckily, she liked everything underneath the fawn-colored Stetson hat Max wore—with no hat-hair dents either, bless him!

For me that's one of the great joys of life—when someone surprises me. Max and Lacey surprise each other and themselves in this story and come to grips with what they really want in life. That made Lacey and Max's story especially delicious for me to write. I'm still smiling about how it all came out.

I love the coffeehouse and the Amazatorium and Uncle Jasper—oh, and Monty Python, too. I hope you, too, laugh and cry along with Max and Lacey as they brew up their own special blend of love at the Wonder Coffeehouse.

And I hope there's a Wonder Coffeehouse in your life where the coffee's just how you like it, the strawberry-rhubarb pie melts in your mouth and all your dreams come true.

Best wishes,

Dawn Atkins

P.S. Look for my first Harlequin Duets novel, *Anchor That Man!*, coming in June 2002.

THE COWBOY FLING
Dawn Atkins

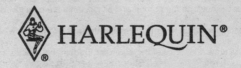

HARLEQUIN®

TORONTO • NEW YORK • LONDON
AMSTERDAM • PARIS • SYDNEY • HAMBURG
STOCKHOLM • ATHENS • TOKYO • MILAN • MADRID
PRAGUE • WARSAW • BUDAPEST • AUCKLAND

To David, who stays awake for the good parts

Eternal gratitude to...my dad, who knows
a thing or two about ranching; my sister Diana,
who laughed at all the right spots; Renata, a Windy City girl
who knows how to Texas Two-Step and wouldn't let my horses bite; Ron,
who can outfit a restaurant in his sleep;
Amy and her razor blades—thank God for your cowboy thing;
Laurie, who, bless her heart, battled her snake phobia to help me;
and Wanda, my editor, who got me here.

ISBN 0-373-25971-9

THE COWBOY FLING

Copyright © 2002 by Daphne Atkeson.

Visit us at www.eHarlequin.com

Printed in U.S.A.

1

"LOOK OUT! IT'S THE THING!"

At the shout, Lacey Wellington rushed through the archway from the café to the Amazatorium in time to see the python slide out of its terrarium, slip over the placard labeled The Thing and slither smoothly across the wood floor heading straight for her.

"Awesome!" A kid bounced up and down in terrified delight, holding the terrarium lid he'd pried off. His mother stood against the wall, pale-faced and rigid as an oak, her souvenir postcards scattered like multicolored leaves at her feet.

"He's perfectly harmless," Lacey said to reassure the woman, then plastered herself against the wall to let the snake pass. Monty Python—as Uncle Jasper called him when he wasn't dressed for the exhibit with aluminum-foil spine scales—was as docile as a cat, but he still was a whopper of a creature and she didn't want to annoy him by blocking his flight path.

With the snake out of sight, the woman snapped to life. "I told you not to touch!" she scolded her son. "I'm so sorry," she said to Lacey, then gripped the boy by his shoulder and hurried him out the door.

Lacey felt a flash of dismay over the lost postcard sale, but she had bigger fish to fry...or rather snakes to snare. She needed capturing tools—and quick, before Monty holed up somewhere she couldn't reach. Her gaze searched the Amazatorium, past the pyramid of gopher skulls, the six-foot-tall tumbleweed, the two-headed bobcat and the furry tarantula, to the wall of gewgaws—mugs, collectible spoons, key chains and pennants emblazoned with the Amazatorium logo.

Then she saw the perfect item—a plastic snake head on a long stick ending in a handle that she could use to open and close its mouth. She snatched that and a tote bag, figuring to grab the python with the gripper and drop it into the bag. Easy breezy.

She raced into the diner, her eyes peeled for Monty. For the first time in the two days she'd been here she was glad the place was empty of customers, so no one would shriek when the snake slid by. The kid and his mother had been the only visitors to Jasper's collection of desert oddities today. Lacey had been making coffee to accompany the strawberry-rhubarb pie—Uncle Jasper's specialty and the only thing he cooked worth eating—when the kid had made his dastardly move.

She stared and squinted, searching the room in vain, until she caught a glint of light off the metal triangles glued to Monty's spine, which made him look like a legless, wingless dragon. He slid like syrup up the back of a booth, across a ledge and then wrapped himself around the neon beer sign above the café's door, his head weaving upward, tongue flicking in search of a crack in the ceiling by which to escape.

Just great. Not only did she have to grab a snake armed only with a gripper and a bag, but she'd have to do it from a five-foot height. She'd handle this, though. She'd handle it all. She'd insisted on no special treatment when she convinced her brother, Wade, CEO of Wellington Restaurant Corporation, to assign her to work at one of their properties. He'd sent her to the most backwater, least profitable of all the restaurants to help her favorite uncle. No special treatment, all right. But that made her plan all the more fabulous. She'd not only help Uncle Jasper, she'd prove herself to her brother in one fell swoop.

It was true that she preferred strategic planning to flipping pancakes—and chasing reptiles, for that matter—but M.B.A.s weren't built in a day, so she couldn't expect her corporate career to be established overnight. To someone with her commitment, a twelve-foot constrictor shouldn't even slow her down. She'd wrestle alligators bare-handed, if it got "corporate acquisitions" on her nameplate.

She'd just consider the snake escape a test of the new, decisive Lacey, who made a plan and went after what she wanted, no matter what it took. She'd handle this snake, all right.

Or pass out trying.

She shoved the stool against the heavy wooden door, clutched the duffel and gripper and climbed up to stand eye-to-eye with The Thing. Monty's foil horns were bent at comic angles, so he shouldn't scare her any more than the exaggerated painting of him on the billboard five miles down the highway, but still...

Taking a breath, Lacey shook open the tote bag, pinched the handle that opened the plastic snake mouth, and slowly reached for Monty. "There's no place like home...there's no place like home," she purred like a snake charmer.

She immediately realized the gripper would be useless for holding the heavy animal and dropped it in disgust. She'd have to grab the snake with her bare hands. She was reaching for Monty when the door banged against her stool. Criminy! She'd forgotten to lock the door against the possibility of a visitor.

"Wait a sec!" she shouted, but the person on the other side shoved harder. The door opened, knocking her stool out from under her. She dropped the duffel to grab the top of the door so she could grip the edge with her knees like a fire pole.

Instead, strong arms grabbed her around the legs. She yelped.

"I've got you." The man's voice was muffled—by her *thighs*, she realized to her horror, feeling his breath through her gauze skirt. Then he shifted her so she flopped over his shoulder like a sack of potatoes. Humiliation and blood pounded in her upside-down brain.

"Shut the door or it'll escape!" she yelled, her face inches from the man's behind. A nice one, she insanely noted, in tight jeans.

The man whipped around and hip-checked the door.

"Thank you," she said with as much dignity as she could muster with her rear end in the air. "Could you put me down?

"Whew," Lacey said when she was finally back on her feet. She brushed her hair out of her face, then smoothed her hand-painted skirt, which now sported an ugly tear. When she looked at the man, he was looking up at Monty.

"There's a snake over your door," he said mildly, lowering his gaze to meet hers. Dark eyes in a Marlboro Man face flickered with male interest, then steadied into amusement. "At least I assume that's what's under all that tin—a snake?"

"It's The Thing." She bent and retrieved her tools and, while she was at it, the fawn-colored Stetson hat that had fallen off the man's head. She handed it to him, noticing his black hair showed no hat dents. She looked at his square-jawed, stubble-darkened face, his broad shoulders in a cotton work shirt rolled to the elbows, and realized she was face-to-face with a *real* cowboy— her first one this close up.

"Thanks," he said, accepting the hat. He gave her a shot of white teeth in a slow smile.

"I was getting him down when you came in," she said, blowing a curl out of her eye with a puff of breath.

"You went after the snake?" For a second, he looked at her with admiration, then his gaze fell on her snake-catching equipment. "What was the plan? Distract him with a puppet play?"

"This is a gripper," she said, extending the toy and flipping its mouth open and closed. Not very impressive, she realized, and the cowboy didn't buy it, either.

Without a word, he put the tipped-over stool against the door and climbed up. He was going to get the snake for her. Double criminy!

"I can handle it," she said, then gulped. "Really."

Her knight in bleached-out denim ignored her and focused on the snake looped leisurely over the beer sign, evidently liking the warmth.

Easily lifting Monty from the sign, the cowboy bent his knees, then stepped gracefully to the floor, a move that normally would have set her female fibers aquiver, but right now just made her feel inadequate. Just like her brother, the cowboy thought she was a bit of fluff who couldn't handle any of life's escaped snakes.

"Thank you, but I could have done that." She felt so guilty about being rescued.

Sure you could, his eyes said. He probably thought she was an airhead, just because she was a woman...and petite...with curly blond hair...and she'd been trying to catch a snake with a puppet. Okay, maybe she hadn't given him much to work with, but she didn't appreciate that don't-worry-your-pretty-little-head look etched in the laugh lines of his cheeks and the crinkles around his eyes.

"I'm more of a strategic planner than a reptile wrangler," she said, so he wouldn't think she was an idiot.

"I see." He, on the other hand, looked exactly like a reptile wrangler, standing there holding the python, his biceps rounded, his abdomen clenched—or maybe the muscles were so firm they just *looked* clenched. Monty had coiled his lower half around the man's forearm, which was tanned and scraped, she noted. He also had a purple bruise under one eye. Probably from a fistfight or some other cowboy thing.

"Where do you want him?" he asked, as casually as a mover placing a sofa.

"In the Amazatorium next door. I'll take him," she said, swallowing a knot that had formed in her throat at the thought. Even though Monty looked silly in his crooked horns, the idea of that muscle of snake flesh tightening on her arm the way it held the cowboy's chilled her.

"You sure?" He didn't believe her, she saw, and that was all she needed to hear.

"Absolutely." She forced herself to grip Monty's width with both hands and lift, while the cowboy gently uncoiled the rest of the snake from his own arm and laid it on hers. As the snake tightened itself around Lacey's forearm, her legs turned to water. Did Monty sense fear? Would he squeeze harder? Docile as a cat, Uncle Jasper said. Trained to be handled. She could do this, Lacey told herself. And she would, despite the doubt in the cowboy's eyes—and her own shaky heart.

With all her might, she willed her wooden legs to move forward. Just another brick in the wall of her success. A learning experience that would enrich her decision-making skills. The squeezing snake was a metaphor for the big chains trying to choke off family businesses like Wellington Restaurant Corp. A metaphor. Right.

Agonizing seconds later, she stood at the abandoned terrarium with her metaphor wound snugly around her arm. The cowboy picked up the discarded lid and waited for her to put Monty inside.

Except she seemed to have exhausted her quotient of courage just getting here. To make matters worse, Monty tightened his grip. He did not want to go home.

"Can I help?"

Hating herself for her weakness, she gave a quick nod.

The cowboy carefully peeled the resistant Monty off her arm, then lowered him into the tank. Close up, the man smelled of spicy soap and clean sweat. Lacey felt safe and hyper-aware of him. An oddly pleasant feeling in the midst of her tension and embarrassment.

The cowboy dropped Monty into the terrarium, and Lacey snapped the lid into place and blew out a breath. "I wasn't holding him at the right angle," she explained, hotly blushing under his gaze. But the truth was she'd chickened out. Period. Disappointment washed through her. She'd failed the first test of her new determination.

"I had a king snake as a kid," he shrugged.

He was being nice about it, but he didn't respect her, and she hated that. More than anything she wanted respect. That was why she was in this sad little spot —to make something of it and herself.

"I'm Max McLane," he said, holding out his hand. "I work at the ranch across the way."

"Lacey Wellington," she said, taking his hand. "I'm from Phoenix, but I'm helping my uncle with the café for a while."

Max McLane had a firm grip and his palm was rough. He was a man's man, as different as could be from the pampered, buttoned-downed Pierce Winslow, the VP of Food Services for Wellington Restaurant Corporation she'd been seeing—with Wade's annoyingly enthusiastic approval.

Unlike Pierce, Max McLane knew hard labor. Honest sweat streaked the sides of his face. The only time Pierce got sweaty was on the racquetball court—and that was useless sport sweat. Max McLane perspired for a purpose.

Lacey and Max looked at each other for a long, silent minute. *Thank-you. Glad to help.* These messages flashed between them, but also something electric that went from the handshake down to Lacey's toes and back again. A man-woman, I-want-you thing as swift as lightning and just as bright. Pierce never made her feel this way—not even in his tux.

Max felt it, too, she saw by the way his gaze seemed glued to her lips. "You probably want to put something on that," he said.

"Huh?"

"The lid," he said. "To weigh it down."

"Oh, right." He meant the terrarium lid, not her mouth. She hurried to the shelf for two heavy scorpion-in-amber bookends. She handed one to Max and they each placed a bookend on a side of the lid. "I guess I'll have to get a lock, too." She studied the glass enclosure a second, then turned to him. "Now, you didn't come to the café to wrestle a snake. What can I get you?"

"Just some coffee," he said. His eyes were intelligent and clear. Free of worry or stress. This man lived a simple, basic life—completely different from her own. Abruptly, those worry-free eyes gave her a simple, basic once-over. He wanted her. Wow! She'd never had such a direct exchange before.

"Follow me," she said, ducking his gaze. "I was just

making a fresh pot when a kid let the snake out." She hurried through the archway, feeling his eyes on her the whole time.

Unfortunately, the coffee decanter was full of cold brown water instead of piping hot coffee. Triple criminy! She banged the ancient coffeemaker. "This seems to be broken," she said, then leaned to look into it, as if that would tell her anything.

"You need to flip the switch under the top box," Max said, pointing.

As she did, the machine hissed. "Oh, yeah. I'm used to newer models." She wasn't used to *any* models, really, but learning how to make coffee, wait on customers and manage the kitchen—if you could call the antique grill where Jasper overcooked burgers and undercooked hash browns a kitchen—would help her understand the nuts and bolts of the family business. That was what Wade had done when he started. She didn't think she should be exempt from the experience, even though Wade thought the requirement unnecessary for her.

"I know it looks like I don't know what I'm doing," she said, as she gathered what she needed to make more coffee, "but I'm a little out of my element." Jasper had gone to Tucson to see about ordering a storage shed for his old art pieces they would be clearing from the café's storage area. She'd assured him she could handle things while he was away. Now she'd gone and let Monty practically escape.

"I don't think anybody's in their element catching snakes," Max said.

"Still, I'm really a businessperson."

When Max didn't say anything, she thought he probably didn't believe her, so she explained more. "Actually, I'm changing the whole concept of this place." She dumped out the water and put a new coffee packet into the coffeemaker.

"Oh, really?" He seemed suddenly alert.

"Yes. I'm turning the Wonder Café into the Wonder Coffeehouse."

"Why would you want to do that?"

"Don't worry. We'll have brand new coffeemakers."

He still looked alarmed, so she said, "And we'll still serve food, except—" she leaned forward to speak confidentially, "—*better* food. Between you and me, my uncle Jasper should stick to making pie." She turned to pour fresh water into the coffee machine. "We'll offer exotic coffees, mixed drinks and fabulous desserts. Plus, we're expanding into the storage room over there"—she gestured at the adjoining room—"so we can have a theater."

"A theater?"

"Oh, yeah. You'll be able to mosey over here at night and listen to folk singers, stand-up comics, poetry readings." When she caught his skeptical look, she realized he probably wasn't a poetry kind of guy and said, "The point is this'll be a hot spot."

"A hot spot in the middle of nowhere?"

"That's the kicker," she said, feeling her excitement rise. "This area's a hidden gold mine. We're close to Tucson, which is fairly hip for a medium-size town, and there's a dude ranch and a health spa not far from here.

Plus, we're right at the crest of the coffeehouse wave. With a little promotion we'll be fighting off the crowds.''

She bent for a coffee mug and saucer, which she placed in front of Max, then looked up to see what he thought of her plan.

He was staring at her chest. Sheesh. Maybe his kind of man only saw women as sex objects, but he could be more subtle about it.

''You got somethin' there,'' he drawled, indicating her breasts.

She looked down and saw a brown swath of coffee grounds across her chest like a nipple-high racing stripe. ''Oh. Gee.'' She scrubbed at herself with the dish towel she was holding. ''Thank you.''

''My pleasure,'' he said, with a sexy edge to his words. He was a rascal, all right. Definitely a love-'em-and-leave-'em-panting kind of guy. She got a little electric zing at the thought. She'd had no idea she had a thing for cowboys, but this one had set off an internal hum—like central heating—that she felt to her toes.

''Sounds like you've got big plans,'' he said, then narrowed his eyes. ''When is all this taking place?''

''We start tomorrow with cleanup. I hope to open in two months.'' The faster she acted, the more likely she'd be able to keep her brother from discovering her plan and ruining the surprise. She poured fresh coffee into Max's cup.

''That's gotta be big bucks.''

''I'm keeping costs down as much as I can.'' She

frowned, a little worried about that really. She had a trust fund, but it wasn't huge, so every penny counted.

"What does your uncle think about this? He owns the place, right?"

"No. He runs the place for my family. And he supports my plan." More or less. He'd refused to consider closing down the Amazatorium and she didn't have the heart to push it.

"Impressive," Max said, though he looked exactly the way Wade would have—doubtful.

"Yes, it is impressive." She lifted her coffee-striped chest with pride. She'd show Wade, all right. And this skeptical cowboy—who seemed more taken with her chest than her ideas—while she was at it.

He took a sip of the coffee. "Mmm, mmm, good," he said, sounding like Andy Griffith in a coffee commercial. A mercy compliment, she saw with dismay, since the coffee looked a little thin to her.

"How about some of Jasper's famous strawberry-rhubarb pie?"

"This is plenty," he said, holding up the cup.

"I insist. Snake-handling is hungry work." Without waiting for a reply she cut a big hunk of pie, nuked it in the microwave and set it before him. "On the house."

He put a small bite in his mouth and chewed tentatively. "It's good!" he said, blinking in surprise.

"Don't sound so amazed. You won't believe the desserts we'll have when I'm finished with the place."

Before she could elaborate, the phone rang and she moved to the end of the bar to answer it. "Wonder Café and Amazatorium."

"What's wrong?" her brother snapped.

"Nothing's wrong, Wade."

"You sound tense."

No kidding. She'd just been through the Great Snake Escape and the Sexy Cowboy Rescue and Once-Over, along with a twinge of self-doubt about her mission. But she'd die before she'd tell him that. "You're such a worrywart," she hissed, turning away so Max couldn't overhear her conversation.

"You're my baby sister. It's my job to worry about you."

"Not anymore. Please." Wade couldn't stop being her stand-in parent long enough to see she was a capable professional. Of course, it was partly her fault. She *had* deferred to his advice up until now. But not anymore. Now that she had her M.B.A.—her certificate of professional approval—she was going to make her own decisions.

"So, how's it going?" Wade asked. "Any problems?"

"Of course not," she said. If you didn't count the running-of-the-snake incident. "What could happen here?" Wade had deliberately sent her to the quietest restaurant of all those the company owned around Arizona so she'd get bored and come home. She'd almost blown up at him until she'd done a little research and discovered what a diamond-in-the-rough the place was. All the better to amaze him with her expertise. Once she showed him what she could do with the place, he'd be kicking himself for neglecting it.

"And Uncle Jasper?"

"Feisty as ever. I don't know where you got the idea

he was getting feeble." Jasper's supposedly declining health had been Wade's excuse for sending her to the boondocks. It also proved to be his ace in the hole, because he knew how much she loved Jasper. After their parents died in a boating accident when Lacey was ten and Wade sixteen, Wade had taken on the role of parent, and Uncle Jasper became the older brother Wade was too serious to be.

Lacey had loved staying with Jasper in one of the tiny trailers beside the café, loved being terrified and enthralled by the Amazatorium's gruesome and fascinating exhibits. Together, they'd played hide-and-go-seek in the diner and gone on scavenger hunts for the rusted tools and machines Jasper used in his sculptures.

Her favorite thing had been watching him work at his found-art sculptures. Three years ago, he'd broken his leg and stopped working on the big stuff—calling it semiretirement. She'd been busy at school, and had hardly seen him in all that time, so this was a great chance to catch up with him.

"I'm fine, Jasper's fine, the café's fine, the weather's fine, everything's fine, Wade, so if that's all you wanted..."

"Hold on." Wade chuckled. "No need to get snippy. I just wanted to remind you we should book the Biltmore for your engagement party. The fall calendar fills up fast."

"Wade." She carried the phone further out of Max's listening range and whispered, "Don't book an engagement party. No one's engaged."

"It's just a formality, Lace."

"Pierce hasn't said word one." Because he didn't think he needed to. Pierce took her for granted, like she was a perk that came with his vice presidency. Actually, it wasn't his fault. They'd fallen into couplehood not long after Wade introduced them. They got along and he was a pleasant companion at social events. There was nothing wrong with Pierce. He was smart and handsome and he meant well, even if he was a little self-involved. But you were supposed to light up when the man you loved entered the room, weren't you? She just felt ordinary with Pierce. Very ordinary. Bored even.

He didn't feel strongly about her, either, she was sure. He liked her because she conveniently filled the "girlfriend" space in his daybook, not because the sun rose and set in her eyes.

"You know he wants to marry you," Wade insisted.

"And what if I don't want to marry *him?*"

"Don't reject the man just because I happen to like him," Wade said wearily. "Pierce is good for you."

"Maybe I want someone who's bad for me." Her gaze flew to Max McLane, swallowing his pie. She'd never thought of eating pastry as particularly manly, but Max McLane was changing her mind. Muscles fanned across his cheek as he chewed and his biceps swelled as he lifted the coffee cup to his strong mouth.

"How can I take you seriously when you say things like that?" Wade said. "You sound like a rebellious teenager."

"Never mind." She sighed. Was he right? Was she just rebelling? Maybe she was being too romantic about love, but she was pretty sure she wasn't in love with

Pierce. She certainly didn't want to marry him. "Just don't schedule anything. I'll talk to Pierce. Right now I've got work to do."

"Work? The only people who stop in there are tourists lost on their way to the Desert Museum. What are you trying to prove, Lacey? You don't need an apprenticeship. There's a place for you here in the company."

"I don't want a little froufrou marketing job."

"You'll do great. You've got fresh ideas. Remember that dinner-in-a-movie idea?"

Okay, she hadn't always been wise. Enthralled by a class in "guerrilla marketing" she'd taken as an undergraduate, she'd turned her final project into a proposal to Wellington. The idea was to combine a movie theater with a restaurant, so people could eat dinner and watch feature films, but she hadn't done enough research. Costs were prohibitive and the logistics impossible. Wade had pronounced it "cute," a verbal head-pat that still embarrassed her.

But things were different now. She had her M.B.A. She'd interned at a software company and a bank. She knew about marketing plans, business projections and project management. She'd even turned down two job offers at high-tech firms because she wanted to contribute to the family business, be part of something that mattered, not just a cog in a corporate wheel. But even that hadn't been enough to change Wade's mind.

"You don't want the kind of headaches I have," Wade said. "Believe me. They paint an idealistic picture in business school. This is the real world. There are pressures and risks. We set tough goals and when we don't meet them, we make hard decisions."

Wade thought he was protecting her. The truth was he didn't think she could handle being on his management team. The problem was he didn't respect her, pure and simple.

Well, she was through *asking* for his respect, she was going to earn it. The hard way. With her own money and her own sweat. When she was finished, the Wonder Coffeehouse would be filled with wall-to-wall customers dipping almond biscotti in mocha lattes, enjoying scintillating entertainment and meeting new people.

Then Wade would welcome her to the management team—grateful for her expertise—and she'd be part of deciding the future of her family's company. But, first things first. She had a pie-eating cowboy to handle.

"I've got to go, Wade. My customers are waiting." Rather, customer.

"Okay, but keep me posted."

"You never quit, do you? What can go wrong?"

"Okay, okay."

"Bye, Wade." She hung up and turned to watch Max McLane. He was just wiping his mouth with a napkin, but he looked rough and tough doing it. And bad. Very bad. He probably had a tattoo. On his chest maybe. Yeah. What did it say? Born To Break Broncs. Or hearts. She shivered and felt heat rise to her cheeks. She definitely had a thing for cowboys.

Max was so wild Wild West, so *not* Pierce. She'd bet he didn't fold his clothes at the foot of the bed before sex like Pierce did. He probably just threw his jeans across the room, the woman across the bed—or the hay—and went at it. Oooh. The idea made her insides vibrate. She'd bet he used women like tissues.

And suddenly, she wanted to be next.

As if he'd read her mind, Max looked up at her from across the room, and smiled a slow, crooked smile. "Anytime."

"What?" She blinked, then realized he'd actually said, "Good pie."

Max pushed to his feet, slapped a bill on the counter, situated his Stetson hat at an angle that made him look so good her heart did a little hop, and started toward the door.

As the door clanged shut behind his perfect rear, she remembered she'd meant for the pie and coffee to be free. She hurried to the counter, snatched up the ten-dollar bill—way too much, definitely a mercy payment—and ran to the door.

"Mr. McLane," she called from the doorway, waving the money, her voice wobbly now that she'd thought of him naked. "It was on the house!"

He turned. "No thanks. With your cash flow, you can't afford any inventory shrinkage."

For an instant she wondered why a man who probably lived from paycheck to paycheck would say something like *inventory shrinkage*, then she got absorbed in the way his swagger emphasized his legs and backside. Criminy times ten!

She didn't know what had come over her, but a woman whose knees went weak watching a cowboy eat pie was not ready to get married, that was certain. She'd have to talk to Pierce and clear the air. Besides, she had too much on her mind with the café. The café and the cowboy. Oh, yeah, the cowboy.

2

THE TASTE of strawberry-rhubarb pie and weak coffee still in his mouth, Max winced as he stepped onto the porch of the ranch house. He hurt all over. No wonder cowboys were bowlegged. Amazing any of them managed to have kids the way the saddle horn messed with a man's equipment. The tumble into the irrigation ditch yesterday had twisted something in his back, and there were still some cholla cactus spines in his butt from the day before. He'd had enough of barbed wire, blisters and cow manure to last a lifetime.

For a fleeting minute, he missed having a nice clean spreadsheet and a snarled budget to work on, but he pushed that thought from his head. He'd wanted out of meaningless number crunching. He wanted the satisfaction of working with his hands like his father had.

As soon as he finished this job and the favor that went with it, he had work lined up with a construction crew to learn the trade. So, just a couple of months of barbed-wire scrapes, boot blisters and bruised tailbones, and he'd be doing what he wanted to do.

Speaking of bruised tailbones, had he left the liniment in the bunkhouse? Buck, the foreman, got a big guffaw about him being such a candy-ass city boy.

Okay, so he didn't have a cowboy's soul. He hadn't known 'til he tried it. And he'd wanted to try.

He stopped in the doorway as a whiff of Lacey Wellington lifted off his shirt to his nose—exotic and fresh, like spicy daisies. He smiled, remembering how good her body felt draped over his shoulder—compact and muscled.

Forget it, McLane. The business he had with Lacey Wellington left no space for anything remotely sexual, except in restless dreams in that fly-buzzed bunkhouse on that rock-hard cot.

Right now, all he wanted was a hot soak and a bucket of liniment, but he had a duty to perform first. He grabbed the phone in the kitchen and dialed the number. In seconds, the secretary put him through. "It's Max," he said to Wade Wellington. "Your sister's settled in here, safe and sound." *And sexy as hell.*

"You met Lacey?" Wade asked.

"Yeah. We met." They'd met, all right. Face to thigh.

"And she thinks you're just a hand from the Rockin' W?"

"That's what I am. And I've got the rope burns and bruises to prove it."

Wade chuckled. "So ranch life's not what you expected?"

"I'm getting the hang of it. I only got tossed on my ass once yesterday." Clint Eastwood he was not. If his luck held, he wouldn't get kicked in the face again by a steer annoyed at having his hoofs checked for rot. Hoof rot, for Christ's sake. Ranching was a nasty business.

Wade laughed. "Good. Truth is, I'm hoping this stint

will get the work-with-your-hands nonsense out of your system, and you'll come back to us. We need you down there."

"Like I said, Wade, I appreciate everything you've done for me, but I'm done with accounting."

Six months ago he'd volunteered at No Place Like Home, a charity that built houses for low-income families using donated materials and labor. Just after his father died, an invitation to participate had come in the mail addressed to his dad, a skilled carpenter. When Max called to decline on his father's behalf, he'd learned that unskilled workers were also needed, so on a whim, and in honor of his father, he'd signed up to be on the weekend crew. He'd loved every minute of it— smashed thumbs notwithstanding—and it had been a way to feel closer to his father.

After he'd seen the joy on the faces of the people he'd helped put in a home, a balanced spreadsheet seemed completely void of satisfaction. He'd wished like hell his father hadn't kept quiet all those years about the joy of his carpentry work. Anxious for his son to get further than he had, Max's father had pushed college, college, college, and downplayed his own work as menial and mindless. So now, Max would follow in his father's footsteps—if not as a carpenter, at least in construction.

"But you're a damn good accountant," Wade said, continuing the discussion they'd had three weeks before, when he'd resigned his job as accounting manager at the Tucson office of Wellington Restaurant Corp. "Why not go with your strengths?"

"I know what I'm doing, Wade." He owed Wade a

lot, but it was time to do what Max wanted, not what Wade preferred or what his dad had expected. Money wasn't an issue, either. He'd paid off his father's hospital bills and his own needs were modest. "Besides, my accounting background hasn't been completely wasted. I did a feed-cost analysis that could save some money in the winter, but Buck's not interested in anything a city boy has to say."

"Don't feel bad. From what I've heard, Buck doesn't respect anybody who can't down a quart of tequila, then shoe a horse blindfolded."

"I think I lost all credibility when I asked him where the nearest laundry was. 'What the hell you doin' changin' shirts?' he said. 'You think them animals care what you smell like?' He's sure I'm gay."

"You should have told him you just wanted to get laid. Weren't you the guy who told me a freshly laundered shirt is one of the top ten turn-ons for women? You were the one guy in the frat house I could count on to borrow a clean shirt from when I wanted to get lucky."

"Consider it my legacy." There wasn't much else he could contribute to the self-assured, trust-funded guys in the fraternity. A working-class kid, he'd been at Claremont College by grace of a scholarship. That hadn't seemed to matter much to Wade and the others, who valued him as a study partner and liked his sense of humor. When they planned ski trips and jaunts to Europe Max couldn't afford, he just claimed family or study obligations.

It hadn't mattered until Heather, of course. Heather

had shown him the uncrossable chasm between them with knife-to-the-heart precision. Max had been okay to play with, but when things got serious—graduation and marriage—she zeroed in on someone who belonged in her world. Max had walked away a better man for the lesson she'd taught him, though: *Always remember who you are.* Of course, he hadn't been that happy about it at the time.

Now he was certain that when he settled down, it would be with someone who shared his values, who knew what really mattered in life. Someone who'd be proud of what Max could *do*, not what he *owned*. Someone who knew who he was, and knew herself, too.

Not that he was looking. He had a new life to explore. He was only thirty. He had plenty of time to fall in love with the right woman.

"Actually, Buck told me he's glad you're there," Wade said, bringing Max back to the present. "You remind him of his son, who used to come out and work the summers on the ranch."

"His son gay?"

"Not so far as I know." Wade chuckled. "Just keep the pumps in your footlocker and you'll be okay." Then he paused. "Seriously, though, Max, it means a lot to me, your keeping an eye on Lacey. Jasper's too absent-minded to be much help."

"Glad to do it," he fibbed, more uneasy than ever now that he'd met Lacey. Max had been glad of Wade's offer of the ranch job helping the shorthanded Buck. He could always use the income until the construction job came through, and the idea of being a temporary cowboy had appealed to him, with all it offered in terms of working outdoors and physical challenges.

Then Wade threw in the catch—he expected Max to secretly keep an eye on his sister, Lacey, until she wearied of making bad coffee and selling tarantula bola ties and came back to a nice safe job in Phoenix where she belonged. He'd made it sound like Max would be performing a public service. Max felt he owed Wade for making a high-paying place for him in the Tucson office three years before, when his dad got sick and needed him nearby. A little bit of secret sister supervision had seemed a small favor for an old friend. From what Max could tell, Lacey did need somebody to keep an eye on her. The woman couldn't make *coffee*.

"So, how's she doing?" Wade asked. "Any problems?"

Max thought about the snake over the door, the plastic puppet Lacey had meant to catch it with and her improbable plan to give the café a makeover. "Headed that way," he said. "She wants to turn the place into a coffeehouse."

"She what?"

He repeated what Lacey had told him.

"Oh, for God's sake," Wade growled when he finished. "That's so like Lacey to come up with some grandiose plan. I should have sent her to the Scottsdale property, where they'd have kept her busy. She thinks she has to prove herself to me. I just want her to have a nice job, get married and be happy. But she wants to be a player. Where the hell did she get the idea that place could be a coffeehouse?"

"She has some theories, it sounds like," Max said.

"Great. Now I've got to be the bad guy and tell her no. How exactly was she planning to fund this little project?"

"She said she had some money."

"Her trust fund. Damn. I can't let her throw that away. Does she even have a budget? Has she costed the project?"

"I don't know about that."

"Has she hired a crew?"

"Don't know that, either."

"Damn."

Wade was right to be worried. Lacey had about as much chance of turning that dusty diner into a money-maker as Max did of winning the rodeo, but he felt like a class-A jerk for squealing on her. He kept seeing the way her green eyes had shone as she'd told him her plan, all the while making him that cup of coffee-flavored water.

"If I stop her, I'll never hear the end of it," Wade said.

"Maybe she'll figure it out for herself," he said in her defense.

"You don't know Lacey. She's stubborn as hell."

He remembered how she'd grabbed that snake right out of his hands, even though it obviously scared the bejeezus out of her. The girl had spunk, that was certain. But she was nervous, too. He'd seen that in the way her eyes darted and in the uncertain set of her pretty mouth. She was whistling in the dark. Not quite as sure of herself as she wanted to sound. And now her brother was going to shut her down....

"Maybe I can talk her out of it," Max said.

"You think you can do that? Let her down gently?"

"Sure," he lied. Him and his big mouth. He was a sucker for spunk...and green eyes.

"If *you* talked her out of it, she wouldn't have to know I had anything to do with it," Wade continued, "so her pride wouldn't make her overreact."

"I guess so."

"Yeah. That would be great, Max. Help her see what a dumb idea it is, and how much happier she'll be in Phoenix, where she has a great job and a future and a fiancé."

"A fiancé?" For some reason, that gave him a pang.

"Yeah. Pierce Winslow. He works for me. And he's a good friend. He's perfect for Lacey."

"That's nice." It was none of his business who Lacey Wellington married, but he hoped Mr. Perfect was good enough.

"Just stay on top of her," Wade said. An unfortunate choice of words that filled Max's mind with inappropriate images. "Be a big brother to her," Wade continued. "My stand-in, since she won't listen to me."

"A big brother. No problem." Except when he thought of Lacey, he didn't want to be her brother.

He hung up from Wade and pondered his new, more complex assignment. Somehow he had to earn Lacey's trust and steer her away from her plan in a way that didn't hurt her pride. How in the hell was he going to do that?

He'd have to get close to her, he guessed. His libido yipped. Not *that* close. She was engaged to a corporate guy, so she wouldn't give a cowboy a second glance—though if he wasn't mistaken, she'd tossed him a couple of speculative looks while he was eating Jasper's pie. He sighed. He hoped the rest of the food was as good as the pie, because it looked like he'd be eating a lot of meals at the Wonder Café.

MIDWAY THROUGH the next afternoon, Lacey dragged a six-foot-high foam ice-cream cone—another of Jasper's sculptures—into the yard and paused to wipe sweat and dust from her face. She was supposed to be *supervising* the cleanup, not *doing* it, but the budget was tight, so she had no choice but to put her shoulder to the wheel. Jasper and his helper Ramón were supposedly working, too, but they kept getting distracted by Jasper's art.

Ramón, a graffiti artist, had been assigned to Jasper as the community service part of his sentence for vandalizing the statue the City of Tucson had commissioned from Jasper twenty years before. Ramón had already served his time—though his "crime" had been more homage to Jasper's work than vandalism—but he'd hung around, acting cool and pretending to be bored, but dogging Jasper's heels like the sorcerer's apprentice. He did some airbrush paintings and swept the café and Amazatorium. When he felt like it.

"I forgot all about this one," Jasper called to Lacey, patting a pitchfork that represented a woman's hair and spine in a sculpture of an embracing couple made of rusted farm implements.

"Fabulous!" she called back. "But we have to keep

clearing stuff out, now, remember? Ramón, can you help?"

But Ramón was busy applying a mist of green paint to the disk-harrow man's frame.

Working mostly alone, Lacey'd barely cleared a quarter of the storage area that was to hold the theater and additional coffeehouse seating. The yard was littered with broken kitchen equipment, antique Amazatorium items and Jasper's old sculptures. The plan was to move the things they couldn't discard to a small storage unit that was scheduled to arrive tomorrow.

Lacey sat down on a polka-dotted, plaster of paris mushroom. Exhausted, frustrated and aching all over, she surveyed the yard's debris. It looked like a tornado had blown through Oz. There was a totem pole built out of fifties appliances, a saguaro cactus made of toothpicks and an oil drum brimming with spray-painted tennis balls. She felt like the princess forced to empty a river with a sieve, and panic surged. Was she up to this? Could she do it in two months? Had she underestimated the cost?

She watched her uncle march toward the farm-machinery lovers wielding an acetylene torch, a wrench and a ball-peen hammer, his steps bouncy, his gray ponytail flopping on his dusty overalls, his face bright with excitement. He'd lit up the minute they uncovered the first sculpture. That was good. He'd been concentrating on small pieces since his broken leg, but obviously his heart was in the big pieces. Jasper was too young to quit what he loved.

It was clear she couldn't expect cleanup help from

Jasper and his little *vato* buddy. She'd have to bring in a couple of helpers in addition to the handyman she'd hired to build the stage, redo the plumbing and install the new kitchen equipment.

She looked across the highway where her gaze snagged on Max McLane working on a Jeep in the driveway of the ranch house. The sight of his strong legs sticking out from under the truck made her heart bump in her chest. He looked so competent, so in charge. A cowboy *and* a mechanic. Mmm...

What was the matter with her? She was panting after a ranch hand, for heaven's sake, when she had a major mess on her hands. The cell phone trilled from her shorts pocket. She pulled it out and flipped it open. "Hello, Wade," she said, trying not to sound annoyed at her brother's second call that day.

"It's Pierce."

"Oh. Pierce. Hi."

She'd planned to call him that evening with a carefully prepared speech. It was terrible to do this kind of thing over the phone, but she didn't feel right two-timing him even with a cowboy fantasy.

"What's wrong? You sound out of breath."

She frowned, feeling that familiar smothered sensation. Pierce babied her as much as her brother did. "Nothing's wrong, Pierce. And we need to talk...."

"Uh-oh, sounds ominous," he said in exaggerated alarm.

"I hate to do this over the phone, but—"

"It's okay, Lacey." Pierce chuckled. "Wade said you were feeling out of the loop on the engagement. How about if I come down there this weekend, take you out for dinner and we seal the deal?"

"Seal the deal? What is this, a merger?" She raised her hands heavenward in frustration.

"You know what I mean," Pierce said. "It's awkward talking about feelings over the phone." He paused, then whispered, "I love you." He paused. "That's what you want to hear, right?"

"No, it's not. This isn't love between us, Pierce. It's inertia."

"Inertia? So this is about the other night. I told you I was sorry I fell asleep in the middle of...things, but I'd had a brutal day and—"

"It's not about sex, Pierce."

"Then what? We get along well. We're decent in bed together—when we're both awake—and we're a good match. What more is there?"

Intense passion, deep intimacy and melding with a soul mate, but she didn't want him to argue her out of her dearest dream. She just knew their relationship didn't come close. "There's got to be more, that's all. For both of us."

"You've been reading too many romance novels, Lacey. Be realistic."

"I am being realistic. Don't you feel something missing? In your heart of hearts? I don't make you crazy with joy, do I?"

"Crazy with joy? Come on. Marriage is a partnership, not hearts and flowers. And you and I would make great partners."

Again with the business terms. "We both deserve

something more. Being here has helped me see things more...clearly." Her gaze whipped to Max's perfect butt—he was bent over the engine.

Pierce didn't speak for a long moment, then he said, "Don't be like this, Lacey. This isn't you."

"Yes, it is. For the first time, it *is* me." She knew what she wanted and she was going to get it. She was still staring at Max McLane, she realized. He threw a wrench across the driveway in what looked like disgust.

Pierce sighed the sigh of the long-suffering. "I'm going to give you some time to get over this."

She didn't want to get over it. "Don't make this harder than it is, Pierce. If you'll just be honest with yourself, you'll realize I'm right."

"Lacey." He tried to sound firm, but she heard a catch of uncertainty, too. He was wounded, she could tell.

"You'll find the right woman, Pierce," she said softly, not wanting to hurt him. "It's just not me." She wiped sweat from her cheek and noticed Jasper, tall and so wiry he seemed made of springs himself, hopping around like one of the shoemaker's elves, banging at a dent in the feed-bucket buttocks of the pitchfork woman. Abruptly, he stopped, wobbled a step, then sat down hard in the dirt. Omigod! He might have heat stroke. "I've gotta help Jasper. Think about what I said. Bye."

Shoving the phone into her pocket, she rushed to her uncle.

"I got a little dizzy is all," Jasper said, waving her

away as he got to his feet. Still, his leathery face was very red, sweat dripped from his small white goatee and his narrow chest rose unevenly.

"We've got to get you in the shade," she said. She could kick herself for not watching him more closely. She knew he was absentminded enough not to notice when he was getting too much sun or working too hard. She led him by the elbow to the café porch. "This is too much strain for you."

"Strain? Hell, no. I'm happier than a pig in sh—...um posies," he said.

Ramón emerged from Jasper's workshop across the yard with two spray-paint cans, but when he saw them, he dropped the cans and abandoned his homeboy strut to gallop across the yard, his face full of alarm. "What happened?"

"Jasper overdid it. Would you get some water and a damp towel?"

Ramón nodded, then bounded past them into the café.

"It feels so good to get at this big stuff again," Jasper said to her. He gestured at the whimsical junk in the yard, then sighed wistfully. "Maybe I'm getting too old for this, though."

"Of course you're not too old. You should do more with your art, if that's what makes you happy."

"You think so?" Was there a tinge of craftiness in his expression? "I did see some great material in a junk-yard on the way home from Tucson. There was a great Gremlin chassis. Not to mention an old wringer-washer rusted to perfection. And the radiators...man, the radiators..." He sighed like Aladdin leaving behind the cave of treasures. "But there's no place to put them. My workshop is way too small and I'd really need some shade if I started working more. Too bad we just bought that one storage unit." Maneuvering. Definitely maneuvering.

Before she could find out more, Ramón brought out the water and a sopping-wet cloth. Jasper drank and Lacey mopped his brow. Once he was certain Jasper was okay, Ramón ducked into the café to find something for them to eat.

"Really, I am too old...," Jasper said to Lacey, his tone begging contradiction. "Even if we *had* more space..."

She sighed and gave in. "I suppose we could get a bigger unit."

Jasper's crystal blue eyes locked on hers. "You know, they did have some of those Quonset hut jobbers of corrugated metal. Prefab and all. A real steal, price-wise."

"Oh, really?" She felt the gentle teeth of a Jasper trap close on her ankle.

"Yeah. It's big enough that I could store these guys and still have room for a nice workshop."

"Jasper, I don't have the budget for another structure."

"It'd be cheap. Minimal amenities—electrical for my tools and lights, but with a good fan system, we could skip the AC altogether."

"I see." She saw, all right. She saw her budget go down in the flames of Jasper's excitement. But she couldn't bring herself to object. And she certainly wouldn't let him work in a structure without a good cooling system. "Give me the number of the storage place," she said on a sigh, "and I'll call about the hut."

"That's okay. I sorta had 'em put it on hold."

"Oh, and I suppose it just might arrive tomorrow instead of the mini-storage unit?"

"Pretty much." Jasper's lean, wrinkled face cracked into a smile. She'd been had, all right. "You coming out here is just the goose I needed, girl. I was sitting on my fanny making pie and knickknacks when I should have been making big art."

Lacey's entrepreneurship instructor would give her a D for diverging from her goal, but "monitor and adjust" was part of every business plan, wasn't it? Besides, making Jasper happy was as important as proving herself. She'd just make it all work somehow.

Ramón emerged from the café with a platter of cheeseburgers. "This is the best I could do," he said. "You got nothing to work with in there, Jasper," he said, shaking his head. "No peppers, no chili, no cilantro, no *chorizo*." He wore his baggy pants low on his hips and his ribbed undershirt revealed several tattoos on his arms—the *Virgen de Guadalupe*, the words *mi barrio* in a heart and the eagle with a snake in its beak from the Mexican flag.

Lacey bit into the burger. "Mmm." She looked up at Ramón. "This is good. What did you do?" Jasper's burgers usually tasted like dried-out cardboard with a charbroiled crust. This one fairly melted on her tongue.

"No *mucho*. I mixed in sausage, seared the meat, then slow-cooked. No big thing." He shrugged.

Hmm. Lacey's business brain clicked into gear. "You like to cook, Ramón?"

"'Sokay. If I have something to work with." He spoke like a fashion designer forced to create with an inferior polyester.

"Maybe you could help out in the kitchen a little."

"I don't know." He looked skeptical, but interested.

"If you're good, I'll pay you."

He looked up at her. "I do the shopping?"

She nodded. "If you're good."

"Oh, I'm good." There was a flicker of pride in his eyes.

"Okay then," she said, holding out her hand. "It's a deal."

His expression sober, Ramón shook her hand. *"Bueno."*

Satisfaction rushed through Lacey. Maybe she'd let Jasper talk her into buying a Quonset hut, and she'd have to hire extra workers to help with cleanup, ratcheting up her costs, but she'd just made a good management decision—reassigning a worker to a job that was a better skill match.

She just shouldn't doubt herself. Whenever she got a hint that her brother didn't have faith in her she got shaky. Same with Pierce. Come to think of it, Pierce didn't even believe she was breaking up with him.

It was definitely over with Pierce. Even if he was good for her, she didn't want him. What she wanted was...her gaze darted across the highway... Max McLane. Yeah. She wanted to sleep with Max McLane. Imagine that. She'd never had a fling before, with all it implied about freedom and excitement. She'd always been in relationships, and not many of those. Serious, predictable, dull relationships, with sex that matched. Didn't she deserve to have an affair? Something as exciting as it was fleeting? Men did it all the time.

How could she know she was ready to settle down if she hadn't experienced wild, fabulous sex? A fling would give her a whole new perspective for when she really fell in love. At least she'd know what she wanted in bed. There was a range of possibilities she had yet to explore. At least she hoped so. Otherwise, she didn't get what all the fuss was about. She was breaking away work-wise, why not sex-wise, too?

And Max would be just the man to break away with. He was a cowboy—the last of the independent men. Having an affair with him would be the perfect way to throw off the shackles of her old life and make her new life real. She didn't want to sleep around or anything. Just one little fling to see what it was like. This would be her own romantic declaration of independence. With fireworks to match.

She would do it. Assuming he was interested, of course. She was pretty sure he was, unless that once-over was just knee-jerk behavior.

Well, there was no time like the present to act. She'd made some business decisions. And now she'd made a personal one. So, how could she make it happen? She could hardly march across the highway and say, "Take me. Take me now." Back home, she would probably just ask the guy to meet her for a drink at the Ritz Carlton hotel and things would go from there. So, transferring that into a cowboy setting, she'd suggest a beer at a cowboy bar of his choice, and leave the rest in Max McLane's manly hands. Before long, she'd be seeing that chest tattoo up close and *very* personal.

She headed to her trailer for a quick shower, her heart racing at what she was about to attempt. This was the new Lacey, she reminded herself, who seized the bull— or the cowboy—by the horns.

And hung on for dear life.

3

JUST CHANGE the air filter and the oil, Buck had told him. That should have been easy enough. Max had worked on his beat-up Karmann Ghia coupe back in college, but the underside of this old Jeep looked entirely different and the manual was no help at all. He tightened the crescent wrench around the plug to what he thought was the oil pan and twisted. Nothing.

He let go a string of expletives, then heard the crunch of gravel and turned his head to see a set of short, chubby toes, the nails painted impossibly pink, in a pair of fashionable high-heeled sandals.

"Whachadoin'?" their owner asked. Lacey Wellington. She squatted and leaned down so he could see her face.

"Changing the oil," he said, holding in his frustration.

"And it's not going well?"

"It's...going...fine," he said, twisting the wrench with each word. The plug remained maddeningly tight. Dammit!

"If that's what fine sounds like, I'd hate to hear you when it's going badly," she said. "I think I heard you swearing from across the highway."

Her good smell wafted to him under the car, making

him go all soft inside. He felt her eyes assessing his work. He'd bet she had an opinion she wouldn't hesitate to share.

"You're going to need something to catch the oil."

Yep. Just like he thought. He sighed wearily. The last thing he needed was a flower-scented busybody whose plump toes looked good enough to eat. "I know what I'm doing," he said.

At that instant, the wrench slipped, the plug flipped out and thick oil splashed onto his face. He jerked away, but not before he got a good wallop of gritty oil in his hair, face and mouth and scraped the skin of his knuckles on the undercarriage.

"Phft! Phew!" He spit out oil. "Ow!" He pushed out from under the car and sat up, shaking the wounded hand he would have sucked if his mouth didn't taste like dirt and used motor oil. "Son of a...sailor! Damn, hell, damn!" He spat some more.

"Oh, dear," Lacey said, springing to her feet. "I'll get something." She teetered into the garage and banged around while he wiped the oil from his face with the side of his uninjured hand. The other one throbbed like hell.

"Paper towels," Lacey exclaimed and rushed to him with a roll.

"I'm fine," he said, scrunching his face against her rough scrubbing.

"No, you're not. You're covered in oil." Her gaze fell on his hand. "And you're bleeding. Let me get the first-aid kit from the café." She thrust the wad of paper towels into his good hand and scampered off in her spiky sandals. He couldn't help but appreciate the nice little wiggle in her backside.

While she was gone he pulled off his T-shirt and scrubbed up with industrial soap in the deep enamel sink in the garage. She'd been right about the oil pan. If she hadn't thrown him off with her perfume and her toes, he would have figured it out himself in a second.

At the sound of quick footsteps he looked up to see her running toward him, a bottle of peroxide and a roll of tape clutched in one hand, a streamer of gauze flying behind her, her breasts bouncing nicely. She could sure tighten *his* bolts in a hurry.

She reached him and stopped abruptly, her eyes wide. "Oh. Well." She seemed awed by his chest, which was strange. He worked out, but he was hardly a body-builder.

NO TATTOO, Lacey noted, but that was the only thing that disappointed her about the half-naked man before her. He had nice muscles, but not overdone, and a flat stomach. Water beaded on his face and sparkled in straight black chest hair that arrowed to his waistband. The hair on his head was smooth, slick and darkly wet.

This could be the perfect moment, Lacey realized—like the scene in an adventure movie where the heroine patches up the hero's gunshot wound and they fall into each other's arms.

"I'm fine. Really." Max held up his hands to ward off her peroxide-soaked cotton ball.

"We have to prevent infection," she said, trying to make it sound sexy—not easy when his eyes zapped all the moisture from her mouth. Her hand shook as she dabbed the torn skin on the back of his hand.

"Ow! Jeez, that burns!"

"Oh, don't be such a baby!" she snapped before she could catch herself. Insulting his manhood wasn't a great start to a seduction. "Sorry." She gently laid a gauze square over the injury and pulled a strip of white adhesive from the metal ring with her teeth. Except the sticky tape slipped from her fingers and landed outstretched on the back of his forearm. "Oh, dear. Let me..." She tugged gently at the tape.

"Ow! That's hair there," he said.

"Sorry," she said. "This'll hurt for just a second." She bit her lip, held her breath and yanked.

He sucked in a breath.

"Sorry!"

"Just don't say that hurt you more than it did me."

This was definitely not going the way it went in the movies. By now, their eyes should have locked and sexual heat should be rising like steam between them. Instead, she'd ripped a swatch of hair from his forearm and he looked so pained she was sure if he wasn't a gentleman he'd be cursing her.

She finished her nursely duties with care, taping the gauze loosely to his fingers. "There. All better," she said when she'd completed the task. She dragged her eyes from his wound to his face, swallowed and tried to suggest going out for a beer, but the words got stuck. Something about the way his dark eyes dug at her kept her from making a peep.

"Thanks," he said, then gestured at the open hood of the Jeep. "I better get back to this."

He wanted her to leave, but she hadn't asked him out yet. She couldn't leave without making plans. "Just don't forget to put the plug back in the oil pan or the oil will just pour out again," she said, to keep the conversation going.

"For a woman who can't make coffee, you seem to know a hell of a lot about engines," he said irritably.

"I took a class once, for your information—Self-Sufficiency for Women. Was the coffee *that* bad?"

He looked at her, then sighed. "No. Sorry to be cranky. I just don't need any help, okay?"

Of course. Giving a macho guy advice on car repair was like walking on his masculinity with stiletto heels.

"I guess I just wanted to pay you back for catching my snake for me."

"Right." Their eyes met and held.

She took a deep breath and started. "I was thinking maybe we could...um... go out...for...a beer maybe?"

"Or dinner?" Max said quickly. "How about dinner?"

"Great." There, that wasn't so hard! She'd asked him out. Of course it had taken an oil spill, a hair rip and an ego bruise to do it, but what the heck. She'd done it.

Jackpot. A rush ran through Max. Lacey had just dropped into his palm like a ripe plum. Over dinner was the perfect time to start talking her out of the coffeehouse. He was so good.

"I'll pick you up at seven," he said.

"Great. The trailer on the left is mine," she said,

pointing across the highway at two mobile homes beside the café. She gathered her first-aid gear in her arms. "See you," she said and tottered off across the highway, leaving his head full of the scent of summer flowers, his eyes full of the sight of her tight jiggle and his mouth full of...motor oil.

He had a date with Lacey. Fantastic. Except he was afraid his enthusiasm had less to do with his favor to Wade, than it did with the way Lacey's tongue had peeked out from kiss-me-baby lips as her busy fingers worked him over.

The night would be strictly business, he warned himself. He was just doing his duty. Suddenly, he remembered something worrisome. He'd asked Lacey to dinner, but she'd asked him for a beer first. Why? He knew what he wanted from her tonight, but what did she want from him? Company? Maybe. Friendship? Possibly. He sure hoped it wasn't something more. Something hot, sweaty and naked. Because, judging by the way she'd yanked that snake away from him, she could be one stubborn lady. And he might not want to put up much of a fight.

IT TOOK TWO showers with industrial soap to get the rest of the oil out of his hair and off his face, but Max pulled up in front of Lacey's trailer in Buck's battered pickup right on time. He'd spent an hour scrubbing the truck, too—cleaning out the hay, mud, horsehair and sweat Buck and the ranch hands had ground into the cab.

Lacey waited for him in front of her trailer in a dress so sexy it stopped his heart. A bright red spandex number, tight as an elasticized bandage that barely wrapped up the goods gathered into a deep vee between her firm breasts and barely reached the tops of her thighs, with come-'n'-get-me pumps to match.

In his experience, the tighter the dress and the higher the hem, the more likely the woman meant to sleep with you. It was simple math. With that in mind, in that get-up, he half expected her to strip him down in the truck. But why him? And why so fast? She didn't strike him as the type who jumped into the sack on the first date. And she was supposedly engaged. One thing was certain. She'd dressed like that to make a statement. And his body had gotten the message, loud and clear.

He got out of the truck and went to hold her door for her. She sashayed toward him in that tight skirt. "You look nice," he said, understating the case so as not to sound like the big bad wolf drooling over Red Riding Hood's goodies. She was a very sexy package, with a gymnast's body—petite, but built—and streaky blond hair that fell in springy curls to her shoulder. The hair, along with her elf-like features and quick movements, made her seem scattered and childlike, until you got a load of the seriousness and intelligence in her deep green eyes. He was a sucker for those eyes....

He held her small hand as she climbed into the truck, averting his gaze at the moment of inevitable exposure.

"Thanks," she said, once she was seated, her skirt revealing lots of creamy thigh. No nylons. Sheesh. And it looked like...yep, no panty line, either. Everything tightened up downstairs. He tried to think about baseball.

"You look nice, too," she said. "Very…um, western."

"Right." He laughed.

"Sorry. That sounded stupid. I've just never gone out with a cowboy before." The sultry way she spoke and the sparkle in her eyes told him that when she said "gone out with" she meant "had sex with." Uh-oh. Lacey wanted to bag a cowboy. Little did she know he was just a CPA with chafed thighs.

He walked around the truck and climbed into the cab beside her, hoping he could keep things cool.

"This is nice," Lacey said, looking around the truck cab. "It hardly even stinks in here."

"Gee, thanks," he said. So much for his hour of scrubbing.

She waved him away from the nouvelle Southwest cuisine restaurant he'd picked out, insisting on "something more cowboy-ish," so he backtracked to a place Buck had mentioned as good for beer and burgers, since the Wonder Café's food was so lousy.

Leo's Cowtown had scarred wood walls, sawdust on the floor, air so smoke-thick you could cut it, a jukebox wailing something country and Stetson hats and cowboy boots as far as the eye could see. "This cowboy-ish enough for you?" he asked.

"If this is where you go," she said. "I want you to be comfortable and all."

Right. She was probably afraid he wouldn't know how to sort out the forks in a place with linen tablecloths. It would have made him laugh, normally, except he was too busy trying not to notice the way male eyes honed in on Lacey as she passed in her tube top of a dress. This was the kind of place where you said things like "Take yer hands off my woman," and got your lights punched out defending her honor. Max didn't blame them for staring, though. With each step, her butt muscles bunched so sexily he felt a dull pain below the belt.

A half-dozen wranglers nursed brews at the bar, their beer guts resting on their thighs. Two more played pool and the booths held more cowboys—none of the urban variety. Other than the three waitresses in short uniforms with frilly blouses, Lacey was the only woman in the place.

They slid into a booth, and Lacey busied herself wiping the beer rings, ketchup and cigarette ashes from the table with a napkin. "So, is this where you guys hang?" she asked eagerly. "After the roundup?"

"S'pose so," he said. Buck kept thanking God it wasn't spring so Max wouldn't be offering up any pie-in-the-sky cost-saving tips on branding and castrating equipment.

"What kin I getcha?" the middle-aged waitress asked in a cigarettes-and-whiskey voice.

"I'm not sure. You order first, Max," Lacey said.

"Shot of Jack Daniels, Bud draft back," he said, keeping with the cowboy theme. "And menus."

"I'll have the same," Lacey piped up.

"You sure?" Max asked. "Boilermakers are intense."

"When in Rome," she answered cheerily.

After the waitress left, Lacey leaned forward, resting her breasts on her folded arms in a way that presented them to crotch-throbbing advantage—perky and swollen as grapefruit with raspberry-bumpy tips. He was dying to touch.

He lifted his gaze to her mouth, which was no less inviting. She had an unconsciously hypnotic way of licking her full lips. Feeling light-headed, Max forced himself to look in her eyes. Not much better. Velvety green with lush brown flecks. He could get lost in those eyes.... Vulnerable. Intelligent, and...

...Scared, he finally saw through his sex-charged haze. She wanted to flirt with him, but she was jittery about it. "Relax, Lacey. We're all friends here," he said. "Don't be nervous."

"I'm not nervous," Lacey said. "What makes you think I'm nervous?" The instant the waitress arrived with their boiler-makers, she grabbed the shot and drank it down in one gulp.

"That, for one thing. You aren't required to slam those, you know. It's perfectly acceptable to sip."

"I...know...what I'm...doing," she said, her voice husky from the harsh liquor. The waitress came back, patted Lacey's back sympathetically, took their burger orders and departed.

Max tossed back his whiskey shot, hoping to dull his senses to the effect Lacey was having on him. The liquor burned all the way down. He banged on the table and gasped for air.

"That's the spirit!" Lacey said, smiling.

He reminded himself that he'd better get started with his task for the evening. "So, tell me more about this coffeehouse deal," he said.

"Oh, you're not interested in that, are you?" she asked, but she sounded delighted.

"Absolutely," he said, clinking his beer stein with hers. "Tell me everything."

"If you're sure," she said, and then she told him *everything*. Right down to the fire-sale café chairs, the velvet remnants she'd bought by the pound for decorative swags and the break she'd negotiated on coffee equipment with a company that Wellington partnered with. He kept getting distracted by the way her breasts surged upward as she leaned toward him, and those lips... He'd love a taste.

"So, what do you think?" she asked.

"Huh? Oh." *Focus, man.* "Sounds kind of risky to me. I mean, sixty percent of restaurants go under in the first year."

"What?" She looked at him like he'd just spoken Swahili.

Oh, right. She was wondering where a cowboy got business stats. "I read that somewhere. I read a lot," he explained. "All those lonely nights in the bunkhouse. Plus, I always keep a book in the ol' saddlebag."

"I see." She gave him a speculative look.

"And anyway, you can get coffee anywhere. Why do you need a house for it?"

Lacey laughed. "You don't go to a coffeehouse just for coffee. You go for the experience, the atmosphere, to see and be seen. Believe me, it's a very popular concept."

He shrugged. "As long as you can bail if things don't work, I guess."

She stopped, her beer stein at her lips. "Bail? Why would I bail?"

"I don't know. I'd just hate to see you lose your shirt, or fail and be disappointed..." His words trailed off.

Her eyes crackled with stubborn fire. "You sound just like my brother."

The waitress arrived and, quick as a whistle, Lacey swept the shot glass off the tray and tossed it back, as if to wash away the thought. "And, believe me, the last thing I need is another brother."

Great. Just when he'd promised Wade he'd be one. "You don't want to down those so close together," Max said.

"I hardly coughed that time." She beamed, blinking water from her eyes.

"I may know nothing about coffeehouses, but I do know about whiskey, Lacey, and believe me, it doesn't taste as smooth coming up as it does going down."

"I'm just relaxing, like you suggested." She grew thoughtful. "I *am* a little nervous. I mean I don't know you very well."

"Don't worry about me. I don't bite. Or at least not hard enough to leave a mark."

She giggled, a sweet, tinkling sound he wanted to hear more of, even if it had been coaxed out by liquor.

"So, tell me more about this project," he said, wanting to distract her from her nervousness so she wouldn't drink herself into a stupor.

For the next hour, he listened to more details about her café transformation, trying to slip in doubts wherever he could. The only problem was that every time he said something negative, she got nervous again and downed more booze. Eventually, her eyelids began to sag and she started to wobble. She was getting schnockered, no question, and it was partly his fault for upsetting her.

"Annnnyway, enough business talk," Lacey said finally, slapping the table for emphasis. "Let's get personal." She leaned across the table, then closed one eye into what was supposed to be a wink, but it came out looking more like a twitch. "I've been going on and on—and *on*—about me," she said, then hiccupped so loudly heads turned. "Now let's talk about *you*. Tell me how you got into the cowboy business." She rested her chin on her palm and gave him a bleary stare.

"The cowboy business?" He hadn't worked up a fake job history for the evening, so he'd have to wing it. "I just fell into it." That was true. With a shove from Wade.

She held up her empty shot glass for the waitress to see.

"You don't want to—" Max started to say, but Lacey's look stopped him. Even the burgers hadn't seemed to soak up much of the alcohol. He caught the waitress's eye without Lacey seeing and motioned for her to water down the whiskey.

"So, what do you like about cowboying?" Lacey asked him.

When it's over. "What do I like…?"

"No, wait!" She jiggled appealingly on the bench, waggling her fingers at him. "I'll guess, and you tell me if I'm right."

"Okay," he said slowly. It was as good a plan as any.

"You love being close to the land, right?"

"Yeah." Except when he got thrown on his keister onto it.

"And you hate fences."

Only when he was the one building them. "You've got it," he said.

"You don't feel right unless you're on a horse."

He hadn't felt right *since* he'd been on a horse. He hoped it all still worked down there. "Mmm," he said, noncommittally.

"And you don't let people get too close. Especially women."

Now they were getting somewhere. Here was the perfect way to ensure this thing between them didn't go anywhere dangerous. Or naked. "You got it. I'm a loner. Absolutely."

"And you like your women straight up, like your whiskey." She saluted him with her shot.

"Those things sneak up on you, Lacey," he warned.

She frowned. "Like I said—"

"I know—you know what you're doing. But do you know how many fingers I'm holding up?" He held out three.

"Never you mind. I feel fine." She gulped the drink and banged the empty glass on the table. "Smooth as water. Now, as I was saying, with sex you like things simple. She wants you. You want her. Honest lust. And when it's over, it's over."

"Yeah..." he said slowly. He didn't like where this was going....

"That's great," she said, holding out her beer stein to clink shakily with his, "because that's 'xactly how I like my men."

Her eyes met his, surprisingly steady and hot. Very hot. A jolt of lust shot straight to his equipment. Holy moley. "That's the whiskey talking," he said.

"Somebody had to do it," she said with a lopsided grin. "I'm not nearly so nervous now." She paused, took a deep breath, exposing an inch more of breast as she did so, and said, "I'm much more com-for-tab-le." She had trouble with the syllables. "So how about it? You game?"

"Game?" He lifted an eyebrow at her.

"For a roll in the hay."

"A roll in the...?" He gulped.

"Yeah. Getting it on. The wild thing. You know—the horizontal mambo."

He shook his head in wonder, chuckling despite the charge he was getting at the prospect. "Lacey, you are something else."

"I just know what I want. And I want you." She pointed at him, but the way her finger wavered and she closed one eye, he'd bet she saw two of him. "You know, I don't think I need any more of those boiler thingies." She hiccupped. "So, do you want me, Maxie?"

Maxie? "You're three sheets—or should I say *shots?*—to the wind, Lacey."

"I'm perfickly fine," she said. "Look, I can touch my nose." She closed her eyes, tilted her head back and extended her pointed finger. It wobbled around a little, then she gave up, dropped her hand and looked at him.

"Never mind. I'm not driving and you're not a cop." She leveled her gaze at him. "Lez quit talking and jus' do it."

He fought the urge to take her up on the suggestion and went for a reasonable approach. "You don't want to get involved with me, Lacey. Like I said, I'm a loner. And a rolling stone. And I'm broke. And I chew snoose and, um, I have bad hygiene."

She leaned forward and sniffed twice. "You smell pre'y good to me. None of that shtuff matters—whaz snoose, anyway?"

"Chewing tobacco."

"O-kay...but not in bed. Anyway, thizzis jus' a fling. We'll be ships pashing in the night. Cazzzz-ual."

"No woman ever means that," he said. "They say 'casual' and the next thing you know they're registering at a Neiman Marcus store." He rushed on before she had a chance to wonder what a ranch hand would know about registering *or* Neiman Marcus stores. "The point is, this isn't going to happen. I can't take advantage of a woman in your condition."

"I'm not in a condition. I'm just a li'l ruh-laxed." As illustration, she let her arm flop like a rag doll.

"Honey, you're practically in a coma."

"Why do you have to be sush a...sush a...genelman."

"You make that sound like something you'd smash with a shoe. Look, I'm going to the john, and then I'm taking you home. Wait right here."

On the way to the men's room, Max paid their tab, smiling to himself. She sure was cute when she was looped. All he had to do was drive her back to her place and he'd be home free—no harm, no foul and nothing to *not* report to Wade.

Except when he emerged from the restroom Lacey wasn't where he'd left her. Instead, she was at the other end of the bar on a stool next to a hulk of a cowboy who was definitely not giving her directions to the ladies' room.

Max walked up to her and gripped her arm. "Lacey, let's go," he said and started to hoist her off the stool.

"Hold it, buddy," the cowboy growled, eyes narrowing. "The lady and me are talking here."

"That's right," Lacey said, completely oblivious to the macho threat in the air. "Randall here's been telling me all about the rodeo and his scars and such. It's jus' fasc-'nating."

"Enough, okay?" Max growled. "Let's go."

"I just ordered the lady a beer, man," Randall said menacingly.

"The last thing she needs is a beer," Max replied, matching his tone.

"What she *needs* is for you to leave her alone." Randall stood off his stool, puffed out his chest and shifted his weight threateningly. Uh-oh. If he wasn't careful Max would shortly be invited out to have his candy ass whupped.

Lacey's eyes opened wide, and he realized she'd finally noticed the tension between the two men. She hopped off her stool, her knees giving a little. "Maybe I should be going," she said to Randall.

"You stay right there," Randall said, blocking her with an arm. His cold eyes stayed on Max and he spoke in a low warning tone, like a snake's prestrike rattle. "I don't like to see women get pushed around."

Lacey's eyes went wide. "He wasn't pushing me around. He was just—"

"Don't let this guy scare you," Randall, Cowboy Defender, snapped. "You sit down and drink your drink, and this guy can take a hike."

Great. The invitation to step outside was about two comments away, Max judged—a prospect he dreaded. His fistfighting days were limited and long ago. It should have been easy to outwit this cretin, but his synapses were misfiring like mad. His brain was Lacey soaked and completely besotted.

He settled for the briar-patch approach. "Okay, pal, you win," he said, in an I-hope-you-know-what-you're-doing tone. He snugged his hat on his head. "I just hope you have your parking fines paid up and your shotgun registered." He leaned close to the guy's ear. "Her dad's a cop and he gets real cranky when his daughter comes home smelling like whiskey. If you get my drift."

The heat in the cowboy's demeanor faded and his jaw lost its lock. "Her dad's a cop?"

"Not a problem really," Max continued, "as long as you don't mind being strip-searched, urine-tested and fingerprinted on a spot-check basis. Oh, and no tattoos. He hates tattoos." He looked pointedly at the eagle on the guy's forearm, turned and started to walk away.

"Hold it!" the cowboy called to him.

Max turned around.

"You can take her," he said grudgingly. "Just don't push her around. I mean it."

"Ooookay," Max said in a long-suffering tone. "Come on," he said to Lacey. "Let's get you home to papa. Got any breath spray in your purse? You smell like you downed a pony keg all by yourself." Max tucked Lacey firmly under his arm and quick-stepped them out the door.

"Smooth, Lacey," he said, once they were outside. "You practically got me slammed into a garbage bin."

"Sorry," she said, sounding chastened. "I didn't realize it would get so macho all of a sudden."

"Good lord. You could float a boat on the sea of testosterone in there." He put his hands around her waist and hefted her onto the truck bench, noting that his fingers almost met around her narrow frame.

She caught his gaze, wonder in her eyes. "So you would have actually duked it out over me? That's so heroic, so primitive, so—"

"Stupid. It would have been stupid. See these?" He gave her his toothiest smile. "I like them right where they are. Next time you want to wave a red cape in front of a meathead like that, get somebody else to shove a sword in him."

By the time he got to his side of the truck he was sorry he'd snapped at her. He glanced over at her as he started the engine. She'd rested her head on the back of the seat and seemed to be pouting about his lecture. It was probably better for her to be mad at him, anyway, so he held the silence.

A minute later, when her head thumped softly onto his upper arm, he realized she hadn't been sulking, she'd been sleeping. She brought with her a wallop of scent—under the whiskey was flowery shampoo, spicy perfume and woman. Automatically, his parts went on red alert. Damn. Testosterone was so predictable.

Listening to her soft breath whoosh in and out, though, eased the sexual tension a tad. Max felt the urge to put his arm around her, tuck her against his chest and rest his chin on the top of her soft hair.

In a few minutes, he stopped in front of her trailer, letting the smell of desert creosote blend with Lacey's spicy woman smell, and the cricket buzz mix with her slow breath sounds. He'd have to wake her up to get her inside. He could only hope she'd forgotten all about her wild suggestion because right now his self-control was worn to a nub...a hot, throbbing nub that made his jeans feel too tight.

"Mmm," she mumbled, then smacked her lips and lifted her head from his chest, a little drool at the corner of her soft mouth. Sweet. "Where are we?" she asked in a sleepy voice.

"Home," he said firmly. "Safe and sound." And to keep it that way, all he had to do was get her inside her door. And stay outside himself. He went around and opened the truck door to help her down.

She blinked sleepily at him. "Oooh, I feel funny."

"You gonna hurl?"

"Hurl? Oh, no. I never hurl," she said primly. "It's too scary."

"You'd feel better if you did. Have less of a hang-over."

"Can't do it." She shook her head stubbornly and slid

off the bench, clutching her handbag. "Whooo," she said and sagged against him.

He caught her and swung her into his arms. This was the second time he'd held her, though yesterday she'd been over his shoulder. This position was much more tempting. Her top had dipped so low that two ripe half moons of soft breast surged upward. *Here we are, come and get us.* She linked her fingers behind his neck and tucked her head under his chin. He began to walk, gritting his teeth against how damnably good it felt to have her firm little shrink-wrapped body in his arms.

"This is nice," she murmured as he walked. Her handbag tapped a rhythm on his thigh. "Like a rocking chair."

He'd like to rock her, all right, and there would be no chair involved.

They reached the door. She pawed around in her purse for a key and handed it to him.

Holding her one-armed, he opened the door, stood her on her feet and propped her against the wall inside. "There you go, Lacey," he said. "Take some aspirin. Get some sleep. Good night."

Her head against the wall, she turned her face to him. "Aren't you going to take me to bed?"

He gulped at the invitation. "Can't," he said and shut the door quick against all that voluptuous woman—a bright red, tempting piece of candy and him a diabetic.

He was about to walk away when he heard a thump and knew she'd slid to the floor. He couldn't leave her like that. He'd have to get her safely into bed. Safely, he reminded himself.

She hadn't passed out, just slid to a dazed sit. Again he lifted her into his arms. The small trailer smelled of her perfume, along with flowers, vanilla and sweet lemon. He carried her down the narrow hall—his footsteps thumping on the thin floor, making the tiny trailer quiver—and into a bedroom barely large enough for a bed and a bureau.

He tried to lay her on the bed gently, but he tripped on something, lost his balance and slammed them both onto the mattress. There was a crack and a thump and the wall side of the bed abruptly hit the floor.

Great. He'd broken her bed.

Quickly, he climbed off her. There she lay on the dark blue spread, a red pistil in a dark flower, so inviting, so soft. She started to roll on the downward slope toward the wall, but he blocked her with a pillow. He looked down at her, fighting the urge to lie down and take her in his arms. What he should do was call Wade and resign his post as Lacey's guardian. He felt like a fox in a henhouse, with a well-built hen offering herself up for dinner.

"G'night," he said finally and turned to leave.

"Don't go," she said, rolling over to look up at him, her curls a halo around her sprite's face. "You're supposed to have sex with me."

He ignored the suggestion. "It's not too late to make yourself hurl," he said. "You'll feel better afterward."

"Aren't you attracted to me, Max?" she asked in a small sober voice. She sounded so sad his heart softened. He sat on the edge of the bed near her face and his fingers instinctively pushed her hair away from her alcohol-fevered cheeks. "Of course I'm attracted to you, Lacey. You're a knockout."

"Good," she said, sounding relieved. "I guess I over-did it. I was nervous about going out with you and then I started worrying about the café...." She met his gaze, heat sizzled, and she put her arms around his neck, pulling herself up until she was pressed against him. "So, let's get started," she said and put her mouth on his.

He stilled against her mouth. Every fiber of his being wanted to do what she asked. After watching her all evening, his self-control was tissue thin. He hungered to taste all of her. His hands itched to slide forward to hold those perfect breasts.

Against his will, his mouth moved against hers. Just a little. She made a helpless sound in the back of her throat. His blood surged and his pulse began to pound in his ears. Uh-oh. If he moved his tongue or hands a millimeter more, he'd be a goner. He'd have her out of that rubber-band dress and be inside her in a heartbeat.

But he'd hate himself if he did. She was drunk as a skunk and he had an obligation to her brother. And anyway, it wasn't really him she wanted. She wanted the rough-and-ready cowboy she'd guessed about over a sea of emptied shot glasses—not a CPA dropout who kept falling off his horse.

With the last of his self-control he broke the death grip she had on the back of his neck, lowered her to the bed and stood up. "Let me get you some aspirin." He thumped down the hall, banging from side to side in the narrow passageway, blood and lust pounding through him, forcing himself to think about the Diamondbacks' pitching prospects to get control below decks, while he pawed through the narrow medicine cabinet. By the time he carried the aspirin and water to her, she was sound asleep. Thank God.

He set the water and pills on the bedside table, tugged her stiletto heels from her feet—noticing those plump toes begging to be kissed—and dropped the shoes on the floor. That tight dress would cut off her circulation, but before he could attempt to loosen it, she wiggled into the pillow, making her breasts swell and him surge, and he decided he'd have to let her blood flow fend for itself. Instead, he covered her with half the bedspread and tucked the fringed edge under her chin.

Well, that hadn't gone well. Lacey wasn't interested in his advice; she was interested in his equipment. He had sudden empathy for the women who said men only wanted them for their bodies.

He sighed. If Wade knew what a bad job Max was doing of watching over Lacey, he'd fire him for sure. For one clearheaded moment in that cricket-noisy night, he realized that would be the best thing that could happen.

4

LACEY WOKE UP with a huge headache and a regret to match. She'd blown it last night. She'd meant to be sexy and alluring. Instead, she'd been so nervous with Max and then worried about the coffeehouse that she'd gotten drunk and thrown herself at Max like a drunken bimbo. *Bimbo* was the right name for a woman who sashayed into a cowboy bar in a minidress and flirted with dangerous rodeo guys with tattoos. It had been one boilermaker over the falls. Or maybe two.

As fitting punishment, she now had a crushing headache, cottonmouth, and for some reason she felt so squeezed she couldn't catch a solid breath. Ah, she still wore her bimbo dress. That explained the lack of blood flow. Then she noticed the world looked crooked and realized her bed sloped toward the wall. Vaguely, she remembered the thud when it had broken.

She caught sight of a glass of water and two aspirin on her nightstand. Holding her head, she rolled slowly toward it, the movement making her brain rattle in her skull. With immense gratitude, she popped the pills and swallowed the water. Where had this come from?

Oh, yeah. Max had done it. She had a vague memory of him saying something about "aspirin" and "hurling," and then lumbering down the hall. *After* they'd kissed. Most of the details from the drunken end of the evening were fuzzy, but she remembered that kiss down to the last twitch. That kiss had had all of cowboydom packed into it—hot and strong, wild and independent, manly and fierce. Ooooh, it made her shiver.

Ouch. No shivering. Shivering made her head hurt. Still, that kiss had been amazing. It had arrowed right through the alcoholic numbness, to the heart of her...and parts below. She'd been right when she'd guessed he'd be nothing like Pierce. He'd been nothing like any man she'd ever known. Pure fireworks.

She had to have more. Lots more. More kissing. More touching. More Max. The only problem would be that after the way she'd behaved, she'd never be able to face him again. That threw a definite kink in her plan to have sex with him.

Max or no Max, the café needed her, so Lacey had to get going. She dragged herself out of bed and into the bathroom. When she saw herself in the mirror, she realized it probably wasn't just chivalry that had kept Max from sleeping with her last night. She looked like an extra from *Night of the Living Dead*. Her mascara was smudged under her eyes, her face was gray and her hair ratted and wild. He'd probably thought she looked disgusting. She'd certainly acted that way. Her face flamed.

She climbed gingerly into the phone booth of a shower and opened the faucet to a gentle stream. Each drop still felt like a needle on her overly sensitive skin. As she showered, the full extent of her screwup began to dawn on her. Not only had she looked and acted trashy, but *she'd* been the aggressor. Big boo-boo. Alpha males like Max McLane liked to call the shots where sex was concerned. She vaguely remembered suggesting they "just do it." What had she been thinking?

Competing in the business world had made her a tad pushy, she guessed. But when you wanted something, you had to go out and grab it, didn't you? Sure. Unless, of course, what you wanted was a cowboy. That required some feminine restraint. You had to be demure, let him make the first move. You could still be a self-actualized feminist and let the man take the lead now and then, couldn't you?

It was just as well, she told herself, as she gently patted herself dry. She should set aside the sex-with-a-cowboy plan for now and focus on the far more important proving-herself-to-Wade plan.

In her tiny bedroom, she tore open the parcel that contained the sample waitress uniform she'd bought in Tucson a couple of days ago. She would wear it today to be sure it was comfortable to work in. Once she got to the café, she'd call in an ad for two minimum-wage helpers to get the storage area cleared, now that she'd lost Jasper to art and Ramón to the kitchen. The handyman was due tomorrow. Moving like a surgery patient trying not to stretch her stitches, Lacey dressed and headed for the café to call in the ads. But first, she'd fix herself the surefire hangover cure she'd learned in college.

The morning sunlight felt like an aerial assault bombing her with brightness, so she was relieved to reach the porch and push through the door. Jasper was nowhere in sight and she smelled something burning in the kitchen.

Cornbread, she discovered, removing it from the oven. An industrial-sized slow cooker sat on the cold stove, its lid open, revealing chopped vegetables and water. Jasper intended to make stew, she knew, but there was no sign of meat. She frowned. Jasper's cooking, such as it was, had suffered a definite downturn since he'd rediscovered sculpture.

She'd round him up after she fixed her cure. Now, how did that recipe go? Tomato juice…two raw eggs…a splash of Worcestershire, lemon juice…heavy salt… and, most important, hot sauce. Lots of hot sauce. Where was the hot sauce? She looked through the spice shelves, then the walk-in refrigerator. No luck. Hot sauce was critical. The burn and sweat cleared the system.

She was still searching when Jasper walked in, his attention focused on what he held in his hands—a metal colander with ice cream scoops of various colors extending like metallic rays from a copper sun.

"Morning, Uncle Jasper," she said. "Your cornbread burned and I think the stew's missing something."

"Oh, yeah," he said. "I forgot the meat." Then he looked up at her. "Oh, and I also forgot to tell you your handyman crapped out."

"What? No!" Thoughts of hot sauce flew from her mind, as did her hangover.

"Said he took another job in Tucson. More money. He was sorry."

"Not as sorry as I am. Now what am I going to do?"

"Don't worry about it," Jasper said, pulling a knife out of the drawer and poking at the colander, not looking at her. "Ramón and me'll do what you need. I told you that." He stopped tinkering and looked up at her. "I'm a little worried about Monty. He seems depressed and his costume's all bent. Did anything unusual happen to him the other day?"

"Uh, not really. We had some visitors." The snake was probably in shock from the Great Snake Escape, but she didn't want Jasper to lose confidence in her snake-sitting abilities. "Maybe he just missed you."

"Maybe. He's got a tender heart."

The door clanged, reminding Lacey how much her head still hurt, and she looked through the pass-through. It was Ramón carrying two grocery sacks. "My tools," he explained, as he unloaded fresh herbs, corn meal and tortilla flour, some links of an orange-brown sausage and a quart-sized earthenware jug.

"What's in the jug?" Lacey asked, removing the cork stopper to sniff the contents. An intense tomato and vinegar smell made her eyes water.

"Fresh chili. Careful. *Muy caliente.*"

Perfect for her hangover cure. Before she could add it to her concoction, the door clanged. With a reluctant look at her unfinished elixir, she headed out to meet the first customer of the day. When she saw it was Max, her heart skipped a beat.

THE ONLY THING worse than having to get up at 5:00 a.m. after a sleepless night was having to get up in a *bunkhouse* at 5:00 a.m. after a sleepless night, Max realized, groaning as he rolled off the cot. Grumpily, he dragged on his jeans. No doubt about it—he was definitely miserable. And he had to ride the range.

For once, he almost didn't mind. Until yesterday, he'd only had to contend with cattle kicks and cactus spines in his butt. Now he had an impossibly sexy woman who wanted to jump his bones. If Lacey came on to him again—sober—he wasn't sure he'd have the self-discipline to resist her. At least on the range he'd be preoccupied with staying on the damn horse.

It was obvious that when it came to watching Lacey, he just wasn't the man for the job. He thought up various ways to explain that to Wade, but no matter how he put it, he'd sound like a quitter. And Max McLane was no quitter.

The sun pounded down until sweat slid down his chest, belly and back in rivulets, strengthening his resolve. He'd just lasso his libido, keep Lacey away from the booze and dissuade her from her plan. He'd have to earn her trust and that meant he'd have to spend more time with those breasts bobbing under his nose. Damn. He'd rather look for hoof rot twenty-four-seven. He'd just have to duct tape his parts. Ouch. There was a lot of hair there.

For a second, he saw her lying in the bed asking plaintively if he thought she was attractive.

Attractive? He thought she was a goddess. Damn.

Okay, so resistance would be tough. Maybe he could work on the other side of the equation—get her to stop wanting him. But how? If she knew he was an accountant instead of a cowboy that would fix it in a quick-hurry, but that would raise more questions than he wanted to answer and might make her suspect the truth.

He could tell her he was gay....

Nah. Lacy the Indomitable would just try to convert him. He could say he was married. But where was his ring? He could tell her he had a war injury and couldn't, um, function. But she'd figure that out in a heart beat...duct tape or no.

No good. What else could he do to zero out her fantasy about him? She wanted to bag a cowboy, but she obviously hadn't a clue what real cowboys were like. Look how she'd cozied up to Rodeo Bob at the bar. Maybe if Max showed her the seamy side of ranching—the sweaty, uncouth, hoof-rotten part of the job. Yeah. He'd head over to the café smelling like dirt, horse and sweat and scare her right off.

They finished up at noon, and Max peeled his aching thighs off Seesaw, the easiest mare Buck had in the stable. He limped her into the paddock, talking to her as he went. "I hope it was good for you," he said, patting her neck, "because it was hell on me." She whinnied at his joke. He'd gotten kind of attached to her.

He checked himself out to see if he was real cowboy enough to give Lacey a reality check. He didn't smell too bad for having been riding and sweating all morning, but he had dirt and straw on his jeans, and his boots were muddy. He'd stopped short of stepping in cow dung. He wanted to chase her away, not make her sick.

For insurance, he reached down for some dust to dab on his cheeks.

Beyond the fence, Max saw Buck shake open his tobacco pouch and extract some shredded leaves. Not a bad addition to Max's act. "Hey, can I have some of that?"

"Since when do you chew?" Buck asked.

"I'm thinking of taking it up."

Buck shook his head and handed him a crinkled packet. "Start slow," he said. "Like the man said, just a pinch between the cheek and gum."

"Great." Not wanting Buck's eyes on him when he tried out the stuff, Max strolled away. Before he crossed the highway, he opened the packet and put a clump in his mouth. Nasty. It tasted like mint, dirt and coffee grounds and was the texture of hay. The bitterness made his eyes sting, his mouth start to water.

Yuck. He chewed as he walked, feeling his heart kick up—from the nicotine rush, he hoped, and not the anticipation of seeing Lacey again. He tried to wipe the grossed-out expression off his face before he pushed through the door of the café. His queasy smile became a full grin, though, the instant he saw Lacey busy at the counter. Just looking at her made his heart bang against his ribs, and he forgot all about the bitter wad of weed in his cheek.

"Hi," she said shyly, giving him that killer smile. She looked so good he almost forgot his mission. She wore a zebra-striped, scoop-necked leotard that clung to the curves of her breasts and outlined her nipples, a mid-thigh-length black skirt that hugged her hips and high-heeled black sandals. A black beret perched on the side of her head. The outfit wasn't deliberately sexy, but she looked even hotter than she had in that come-and-get-me minidress the night before.

"Hi, yourself," he said, alarmed to hear a lusty undertone in his voice.

"I'm trying out the waitress costume to make sure it's comfortable," she said. "Does it look okay?" She turned around slowly to give him the full treatment. And it was a treatment, all right. The sandals made her calf muscles bunch into firm balls—like a dancer. He imagined her naked except for those heels...and maybe the beret...and his heart began to pound faster than it already was with the nicotine pumping in his veins.

"I got a great price on these leotards. Castoffs from a ballet troupe. They match the fabric I'm covering the bar stools with. The skirt's not too short, is it? I don't want the girls to feel ogled. What do you think?"

"What do I think?" *I think I want to strip you down and jump you.* "I think it looks nice," he said, gulping a bitter swallow of tobacco juice.

"Heels won't work, though," she said. "They'll need flats because of all the walking." She caught her bottom lip with her teeth in that riveting way she had. He fought a surge of blood. Damn, damn, damn it to hell.

He had to say something about last night, make it clear that it had been a mistake....

They both spoke at once. "About last night—"

They smiled at each other.

"Go ahead," she said.

"Ladies first."

"Okay. I wanted to apologize. I know I was a little, well, tipsy...."

"Tipsy?" He chuckled. "You were plastered."

"Okay, I was plastered. Let's not make a big deal of it."

He held up his hands to show he meant no harm. "You bet. Whiskey under the bridge."

"Good." She nibbled on her lip.

God, he wished she'd quit that.

"I mean," she continued, "I don't normally act so... um, you know...I don't usually..."

"Come on like gangbusters?"

"Gangbusters?" She frowned. "I wasn't *that* bad."

He lifted an eyebrow at her. "'Let's quit talking and just do it?'"

"So I wasn't subtle. Next time I'll stick with white wine spritzers."

Next time. There would be no next time, Max vowed, if he had any say—or self-control—about it.

"Can I get you some coffee?" Lacey asked.

"That'd be great." Hopefully, it would take the taste of tobacco out of his mouth. The stuff had numbed his tongue, made him a little dizzy and his stomach wasn't too happy about the juice he'd swallowed. Intense. No wonder Buck was always spitting in the dirt or an empty can. "You got a paper cup handy?"

"Sure," she said. She poured his coffee and went to the far end of the counter for a foam cup.

Spitting snoose into a cup would be a perfect illustration of the unsavory side of cowboying. Plus, he needed to get rid of it fast. The smell of greasy food was adding to his nausea. He'd only had a piece of jerky and a fist-ful of smoked almonds this morning.

She handed him the cup. He spit the juice and most of the tobacco into the cup, then looked up at her and grinned. "Nasty habit, huh?"

"Kind of messy." She scrunched up her nose, and looked so cute he wanted to kiss her. Luckily his mouth was filled with mulch, so it was easy to resist the impulse.

She studied his face. "Looks like you've been really working hard today."

He remembered he'd rubbed dirt on himself. "Oh, yeah. That's the cowboy life. Smelly and dirty. I get so used to it I hardly notice it anymore." She'd noticed the grunge factor. Good The only problem now was the threatening way his stomach roiled and cramped. Hurling was not out of the question. "Maybe I should leave?" He made as if to get up.

"Nonsense." She put a hand on his arm. "You're a working man. You're fine with me. Can I get you some lunch?"

"Nah. I'm not ready for lunch yet." His stomach was too unsettled to even consider food.

"Breakfast then? Jasper's AWOL, but I can make you some scrambled eggs."

"No, that's okay."

"I insist. It's on the house. As an apology for last night," she said, heading for the kitchen. She stopped at the swinging door and turned to him. "Bacon or sausage?"

The thought of either made him want to gag. "Just the eggs," he managed to choke out.

While she was gone, Max tried to wash down the tobacco taste with coffee, but that made his stomach even more upset. By the time Lacey slapped the plate under his nose, the smell of the eggs and the sight of the sausages she'd included—their grease still bubbling—made Max's stomach lurch upward. He shoved the plate to the side.

"They look that bad?" Lacey said miserably.

"No. It's fine. It's me. I'm a little queasy."

"Oh, of course, you're hungover!" Lacey said, sounding, of all things, delighted. "I've got just what you need."

A stretcher?

In a minute, she was back with a damp cloth and a glass of what looked like brown tomato juice. She set the glass down and began to wipe his cheeks and forehead with the wet rag. "Whew! You must have had to wrestle a cow to the ground judging from all this dirt."

She had the greenest eyes and she was so close and she was leaning forward, so her breasts surged out of the zebra stripes, screaming *touch me, kiss me, take me home*. This was torture, especially with his stomach still threatening to clean house.

"Drink up," she said, handing him the ominous-looking drink. "It's the best hangover cure. You need it more than me."

"But I'm not—" He started to tell her he wasn't hungover, but he couldn't tell her he was a snoose virgin, so he just gave in and took the glass from her. How bad could it be?

Yow! Liquid fire licked down his throat. "Oh...my...God," he gasped. He pounded the counter and rasped out, "Water." His eyes poured tears. His nose burned and the stuff blazed a magma trail to his already-burning stomach.

She poured him a quick glass of water and handed it to him. "That's the hot sauce you're feeling. The heat burns off the hangover." She watched him gulp down water, looking hopeful. "Is that better?"

He panted. "Sure. Better." Too soon to tell. His stomach was too stunned to react yet.

"Looks like I'm always having to fix you up," she said affectionately. "You're going to have to start calling me Nurse Lacey."

Nurse Lacey? More like Lacey de Sade. The hair on his arm might never grow back and now he wouldn't be able to taste anything for weeks. Hell, he wouldn't be able to swallow. His stomach had probably been burned completely away. "Thanks a lot," he choked out.

"My pleasure," she said, purring the word seductively. She leaned a little closer, giving him an appealing shot of cleavage.

Damn. Looked like his smelly, dirty, tobacco-spitting cowboy act had had no negative effect on Lacey. But it was *killing* him.

COULD THE MAN *be* any more sexy? Lacey asked herself of Max, as she watched him catch his breath from her hangover concoction. She might have put a little too much hot sauce in. He smelled of clean sweat and outdoors and his muscles were so taut and perfect. Those smears of dirt on his cheek had looked like war paint. She'd hated to wash them off. He looked so hot.

Just being this close to him made her feel shaky all over. But she wouldn't do anything or say anything. She'd let him come to her. It was tough though, when he stared at her like he had when he walked in—like he saw right through her clothes and itched to touch.

She had to be strong, stay feminine and demure, and pretty soon Max would make a move. Before long they'd be going for a roll in the hay—maybe literally. Though hay was probably pretty itchy and full of bugs. She'd just leave the decision in his hands—retaining veto rights, of course. Letting the man run the show only went so far....

Just then, she heard the roar of a large truck motor and looked out the window to see a huge rig pull up. The bed of the trailer held stacks of curved sheets of metal and big planks of plywood. She hurried outside to find Jasper hoisting himself onto the truck bed.

She called up to him, "Is this what I think it is?"

"Sure is. It's the Quonset hut."

"But it's all in pieces."

"That's why it was cheap," he called down to her. "Can you brace this while I lower it." He lowered one of the curved pieces of metal.

"Wait a sec, Jasper. First, let's figure out where you're going to build the thing," she said.

But Jasper either hadn't heard, or was ignoring her

because a hunk of curved metal was on its way down to her. She braced the metal as Jasper lowered it, backing up as she went. As it hit the ground, she bumped into something solid and warm—Max's chest.

"Can I help?" Max said, his voice deep and reassuring in her ear.

"Who's this?" Jasper asked, stopping his efforts to look at Max.

"Max McLane," Max said. "I'm working at the Rockin' W." He extended a hand.

"I'm Jasper Wellington," Jasper said, reaching down to shake. "Nice to meet you, young man. You feel up to lending some muscle here?"

"Glad to. If you'll hang on a minute, I think I can figure out something for you."

Jasper considered his words, then nodded and sat down on a pile of plywood in the truck bed to wait.

Max walked the length of the trailer bed counting. Then he stepped out in the yard and looked around, then up at the sun. Then he walked back to them. "Judging from what's here, this will be about five hundred feet long and fifty feet wide. You'll want it over there—" he pointed a few yards to the north of the café— "where the mesquites will shade the western face." He told the driver where to move the truck.

Lacey started to follow the truck with Max, but he stopped her. "I'll help Jasper. You can go back inside if you want," he said.

"This is my project. I'll do what has to be done."

"You sure? You'll get your, um, outfit, dirty." He

glanced at her chest, then away, uncomfortable noticing her, she guessed.

"Of course. I'm on it. All of it—chasing snakes or unloading a do-it-yourself art studio. Besides, it'll take both of us to slow Jasper down before he gets heatstroke." She pointed to where her uncle was hopping across the truck bed, cheerfully flinging pieces of metal to the ground.

Ramón came out of the kitchen to help them, and before long the place looked like a silo had exploded in the yard, and Jasper had begun bolting the pieces together.

As Max had predicted, Lacey's waitress costume was dusty and streaked gray from metal shavings. Her arms ached and she was drenched in sweat. She'd long ago ditched the sandals for more practical shoes.

"I need you to sign here...and pay," the truck driver said, handing her a clipboard.

She looked at the price and had to restrain a gasp. If this was cheap, she'd hate to see how much the preassembled version would have cost. This would take a big bite out of her renovation budget.

She went into the café to write the check and when she handed it to the driver, she felt Max's eyes on her.

"Steep?" he asked when the truck had driven away.

"Triple what I expected," she said on a sigh. "It doesn't matter, though. I've never seen Jasper so happy." They both watched Jasper gleefully welding away, with Ramón's lethargic assistance. "This is his heart's desire—to have a space to work and a place for his art. At least I won't have to worry about him getting heatstroke working in the sun on the big stuff. That makes it worth every penny." She tried to smile. Then she called out to Jasper and Ramón, "Take a break. I'll go get some iced tea."

"I'll help," Max said and walked with her to the café. She felt good with him at her side. She'd managed not to do anything the least bit aggressive so far and their fingers had tangled a couple of times as they helped unload the sheet metal—using a ramp and hand truck at Max's suggestion. On the other hand, sweat and dust had surely masked whatever sex appeal she had.

In the kitchen, she took a jar of iced tea from the walk-in refrigerator.

"I'll get the glasses," Max said.

"You just sit. You've already done too much. You worked all morning at the ranch and then helped us." She filled four tall tumblers with ice and placed them on a tray with the pitcher of tea. "I really appreciate what you did out there," she said as she worked. "If you hadn't figured out the placement of the hut, we'd have had sheet metal strung from one end of the property to the other." She filled two of the glasses and handed him one. Their fingers linked, their eyes met. "You were pretty fast with the figures," she said softly.

"I'm good with math. No big thing," he said equally softly, then took a long swallow of tea.

A cowboy, a car mechanic *and* good at math. Max was a regular Renaissance man. And that gave her a brilliant idea…. "Would you be my handyman?"

"What?" Max choked on his tea and banged the glass on the table.

"I just lost the guy I hired and I desperately need help. Could they spare you at the ranch for a while? I'd try to match your wages. What do you think?"

She thought it was the perfect solution to both her problems. Max would undoubtedly be a great handyman—look how well he handled the hut unloading. Plus, working together—rubbing shoulders...and elbows...and who knew what else—would surely lead to nature taking its course.

"Oh, no. I don't think so," Max said, shaking his head a little too fiercely. "I mean, Buck's shorthanded."

"Oh. That's too bad." He seemed relieved to have an excuse. Did he think she'd be a terrible boss? Feeling glum, she drank her tea.

"Maybe this isn't a good time to do the renovation," Max said. "I mean, if money's tight and you can't hire anyone."

"It's a perfect time.... It's the only time, really." She set her jaw. "I'll make it work somehow."

He held her gaze, testing her somehow. It was strange the way Max kept worrying about the café makeover. "If things don't work, there's no shame in changing plans," he said.

What was going on here? He'd tried to discourage her the night before, too. Did her doubts show that much? "The budget's a little tight, but I'll just cut back on promotion and some of the amenities. And I'll be able to hire someone, I'm sure. I have to make this happen. Now."

His eyes held hers, dark and intense. Then he surprised her by reaching out a hand to touch her face.

"Looks like you got a little dirt..." he said, slowly brushing his fingers across her cheekbone. Very slowly. His touch was surprisingly gentle.

"Thanks," she whispered.

"You're always cleaning *me* up. The least I can do is return the favor." He smiled. "Your skin's so soft," he said, almost as if he couldn't help himself. Was that desire she saw in his dark eyes?

Their gaze held for a long minute...the tension mounted... Max leaned toward her, tilted his face.... Omigod! He was going to kiss her. At last. She closed her eyes and waited, trembling a little. She wasn't drunk this time, so she would feel every iota of contact. She couldn't wait. His warm breath brushed her face, smelling of iced tea and mint and something manly—the tobacco, probably. She leaned in....

"I'll do it," Max said abruptly.

Do what? Ravish her right here in the kitchen? Her eyes flew open in delighted anticipation.

"I'll be your handyman."

"You'll what?"

"Buck can probably spare me in the afternoons."

"Oh. Well. That's great." The good news almost made up for the fact that he wasn't going to toss her onto the stainless steel worktable and go at it. Now she would have a competent handyman and maybe, just maybe, something more. "Okay then. Give me a little bit to get cleaned up, then I'll walk you through the café to show you what I plan. This will be perfect."

Perfect. Right. Max couldn't believe the words that had just popped out of his mouth. He was just supposed to talk her out of her plan, not be her *handyman*. God. That sounded like something from a porn flick. *Oooh, baby, is that a hammer in your pocket or are you just glad to see me?* Even worse, he knew slightly less about being a handyman than he did about wrangling. His experience on the construction site at No Place Like Home had consisted of doing what he was told—hammer this, caulk that, hold this in place. What was he getting himself into?

It didn't matter. Lacey needed help, and he'd been powerless under the spell of those green eyes. If she'd asked him to hang upside down from the stove hood and screech like a monkey, he'd have asked, howler or spider?

Oh, well. This would give him a chance to get a look at her...his gaze strayed to those soft green eyes, then dropped to her chest...*budget*. Yeah, he needed to look at that. So, what the hell... He'd just think *duct tape*.

5

THE ONLY THING Lacey could think as she watched Max enter the diner an hour later was *cleans up nice*. He looked so good in jeans and a denim shirt, his face fresh-shaven, his Stetson hat at that sexy angle. He had that great cowboy swagger that made him look built to ride horses. Those tight jeans didn't hurt the effect, either.

She'd gone for an innocent, but sexy look herself, choosing a silk spaghetti-strapped blouse with denim shorts. Max's gaze zipped up and down, like he was trying not to stare, but couldn't help himself. Perfect.

"Let me introduce you to the new Wonder Coffeehouse," she said with a sweep of her arm. "I'll tell you my ideas and you give me your feedback on the logistics."

She tried to walk next to him as she led him to the storage area, but he hung back, acting like a nun had hung a yardstick between them at a dance. It was weird. She could only conclude that her Zena-Sex-Queen behavior the night before had really turned him off...though there had been a definite mutual-lust vibe when he'd touched her face over the iced tea.

She forgot about that, though, as she began to show Max her dream. In the emptied-out storage room she pointed out where the stage would go and the bar, then led him to the kitchen to talk about the new sink, worktables and dishwasher.

Over the next half hour, though, her enthusiasm faded and her irritation rose as Max gave her nothing but "yeah, buts." As in, "Yeah, but a second sink means more plumbing. Yeah, but the fire marshal won't like that many tables. Yeah, but your wiring is too old to accommodate more appliances."

When he wasn't giving her "yeah, buts" he was making cash register noises about everything. He claimed he was just trying to save her money, but all the tsking and head-shaking bummed her out. Eeyore goes construction.

They finished up in the Amazatorium. "I'd like to spruce this place up a bit," she said, "but it's Jasper's touchstone, so I guess I'm stuck with a two-headed bobcat and the world's largest tumbleweed."

"But that's what's cool about the place," Max said—the first encouraging comment he'd made so far. "In fact, the whole place is great the way it is. Maybe you could just improve the food, redo the highway sign and call it renovated."

She stopped and faced him, her hands on her hips, her throat tight with frustration. "I'm sure you're trying to be helpful, Max, but I wish you'd trust my judgment a little. I've studied restaurants, remember? I know what I'm doing."

"Sure, sure. It's just that when you figure the costs for new restaurant equipment, plus the cost of labor—"

"Please. You're starting to sound like an accountant."

From the look on his face, it was as though she'd just accused him of being an ax murderer. "Oh, no. I'm not *that*," he said. Strange. "I'm just remembering what happened to my friend who owned a restaurant. He got in over his head and—"

"I'm not getting in over my head, okay? It's nice you're so concerned, and, believe me, I have some worries, but I'm on top of them. I don't need two people worrying about it." She blew out a breath. "I'll handle the budget, you handle the building and we'll be fine."

"Okay," he said with a shrug that said: *It's your funeral.* She wondered briefly whether it had been a mistake to hire him. No, she was sure he'd do a good job. She had good hiring instincts and Max was a multitalented guy.

"Let's go over to my place and I'll fix us something to eat. We can make a supplies list so you can hit the Home Depot store tomorrow. And I promise you can be really, really thrifty."

Once at her trailer, Max hesitated at the threshold, but she urged him inside, then left him on the sofa with a pad and a calculator, while she went into the kitchen to rustle up a meal. There wasn't much in the fridge. She opened a bag-o-salad and slapped a couple of diet frozen dinners into the microwave, then carried out a bottle of beer for Max and a white wine spritzer for herself to prove she wasn't going to get plastered and attack him again.

Max sat straight up on the couch, like a first date on his best behavior with the girl's parents, the pad on his lap.

"Dinner will be ready in a flash," she said and sat next to him. "What have we got so far?" She leaned in to see what he'd written. She was close enough to see the muscle in his neck and catch the musk of his skin mingling with his aftershave—spicy and masculine.

His strong fingers stilled on the pencil. "I thought we'd start small," he said, turning to catch her gaze. Their eyes locked. The familiar tension rose.

"Sounds good," she whispered, unable to keep from sounding sexy. Her heart began to pound.

"And then gradually grow," he said in a similar tone.

She tried not to check his lap to see what else might be growing. Instead, she kept her eyes on his face. His lips were perfect—strong, but sensuous. She remembered how right they'd felt the night before. "D-d-do you think that's enough, um..." she licked suddenly dry lips and pointed a trembling finger at one item he'd written, "wallboard."

"Plenty," he whispered.

She remembered how his fingers had dug into her ribs last night. He'd been trying to restrain himself, she'd known, even through her alcohol haze. She couldn't help imagining what it would be like if he let go, did what he wanted. Right here. Right now.

"That's good then," she said, lust making her woozy.

Max's eyes closed for a second. He had to be feeling the same charge she was. He opened his eyes and looked straight at her. "I need to see..." he said slowly. His gaze lasered from her eyes to her mouth.

"You need to see...?" she repeated.

"Your..." His gaze circled her breasts, then moved lower.

"My...?" She swallowed hard.

He cleared his throat. "Budget," he finished firmly. "I need to see your budget."

"My what?" She woke from her seductive haze. "Oh. My budget. Sure." Damn. The man was made of *stone*. She blew out a frustrated breath and went to fetch the folder with her calculations and research. Stone, steel, ice. He was hard in every way except the one she wanted.

She marched over to him and dropped the folder in his lap. "There. My budget. Demographics. Research. Profit-loss projections. Everything." She plopped onto the far end of the sofa and crossed her arms. He wouldn't have a clue what that all meant—he was a cowboy, not a businessman—but maybe it would finally convince him she had everything under control.

Max flipped through the folder, poring over the pages like he actually understood them. He referred back and forth from one to another, wrote things down, made "hmm" noises like a doctor with a puzzling diagnosis.

All the while, her anger grew at his assumption she was screwing up. Just like Wade, he believed the worst about her. Max had no reason whatsoever to doubt her. Unless he was picking up on her own doubts.... She hated that thought, so she sat there feeling steam rise around her while Max flipped the pages.

Finally, he closed the folder and looked up at her. "This is good," he said.

"Of course it's good. I've been trying to tell you that for hours. I'm not an idiot. Of course I have concerns. The budget's tight, I'll have to cut corners. I'm not oblivious to the risks. But I know this will work." She couldn't hide her anger.

Max's face softened. "Look, Lacey, I'm not trying to give you a hard time. I just don't want you to make a mistake."

"I won't. I can't afford to. Too much is riding on this for me. You don't know what's at stake."

"Then tell me, Lacey. Tell me what's at stake." His eyes held her gently, but with intensity, telling her he really wanted to know. Part of her knew that was odd. They were virtual strangers, after all, and even if they ended up in bed together, they wouldn't get to the "tell me about your childhood" part of a relationship. This was to be a ships-passing-in-the-night thing. But since the moment they'd met, Lacey had had the strange feeling that Max understood her, as if he already knew a lot about her, almost knew what she was going to say before she said it.

So she told him. She was too upset *not* to. She told him about Wade being a father to her after their parents died, and how he didn't trust her, and how she'd always deferred to him until now, when she wanted to earn his respect more than anything.

"If you know you're good, why do you care what Wade thinks?"

"Because I want to be part of our family's company. And I want to make a difference that matters. I want to show Wade I'm capable of doing something on my own. I don't want Wade to *give* me a job. I want to earn it. I want him to see I'd be wasted in the marketing department designing coupons. I want him to realize I have a bigger contribution to make."

Max was silent, pondering her words. "So this is a real big deal then."

"It's my dream, Max. You probably don't understand because you're already living your dream. But this one's mine."

He looked at her a long time, as if he had a decision to make, as if something vital hung in the balance. Then, holding her gaze in his, he said. "Okay, I'll help you."

She laughed a little. "You already said you'd work for me. Don't take it so seriously. It's not like your career's at stake or anything. It's just a job."

"Right."

"You're my handyman, remember?"

"Your handyman. Right."

"*I'm* the one whose career's at stake." She almost couldn't laugh.

"ARE YOU trying to tell me I should let her do it?" Wade asked when Max reached him the next day.

"Yes. That's exactly what I'm trying to tell you," Max said on a sigh. "She's slightly undercapitalized and her marketing plan's weak—the property's off the beaten track—but with a boost, it could take off." He explained what he'd gleaned from the papers he'd studied.

"Boutique properties are not in our strategic plan," Wade said. "I was going to close the café when Jasper retired."

"Didn't you tell me once that you thought Wellington ought to diversify?" Max decided to focus on the business side of things to appeal to Wade, though it was really Lacey he was worried about.

Lacey Wellington had whammied him again, Max had realized while heading back to the ranch after eating half-frozen chicken l'orange and wilted lettuce, his jeans tight from spending two hours in close proximity to all that woman. She hit him like two boilermakers in thirty seconds—wham, bam and he was putty in her hands.

First, he'd agreed to be her handyman—a job he was clueless about—and now he was trying to convince Wade to let Lacey renovate the café. Luckily, her plan looked really good, because he knew he'd have helped her anyway, after the way she'd talked about it, her face bright with excitement and hope, eager to get started...and a little scared. His heart had squeezed into a fist seeing how much this meant to her. So, here he was talking to Wade.

"She'll be really disappointed if I shut her down," Wade said, surprising Max with his attention to Lacey's feelings.

"It would break her heart."

"Can't you talk her out of it?"

"I've spent hours trying. Finally, I offered to be her handyman so I had an excuse to look at her plans." No point in throwing in that he'd only blurted the offer just to keep from kissing her. "And I was damned impressed. From a business standpoint, that is." The personal standpoint was a whole new ballgame.

"It could be an interesting experiment. If the numbers look all right..." Wade paused and Max held his breath. "Oh, hell, get me copies of what she's doing and I'll look it over. If it seems workable, I won't interfere."

Relief and pleasure washed through Max. Great. Now he wouldn't be responsible for breaking Lacey's heart. Even better, he'd just discharged his duty to Wade. He could resign the ridiculous handyman job he told Lacey he'd take—find her a substitute, maybe— finish out the blasted ranching job and then head back to Tucson, bloodied, bruised and barbed-wire scraped, but with his honor still intact, since he'd refrained from sleeping with Lacey.

"Of course you'll manage the project," Wade said, snapping Max's attention back to the conversation.

"Huh?"

"Contain costs, make sure she doesn't go over budget."

"That's not really necessary," he said, his mind racing. He had to get out of this. "She's perfectly capable and—"

"I need someone to keep tabs on the project and I can't come down there. You're already working for her, aren't you? So you're perfect. You can supervise things. Subtly."

"I can?" he said weakly.

"I'd think you'd want to. I'll be approving this on your say-so, Max. I need to count on you for follow-through."

"Sure," he said. "I'd be glad to help." *On what planet?* Here he was again, dragged back to Lacey. He seemed to be the victim of some kind of undertow tugging him closer and closer. He was just scared he'd get tired of dog-paddling and go with the flow. Straight into trouble.

A WEEK LATER, Lacey sat at the card table she'd set up in the middle of the expanded seating area of the coffeehouse so she could answer her workers' questions and help out where she was needed—but mostly to watch the Wonder Coffeehouse grow before her eyes.

She loved hearing the power saw buzz and the hammers pound.

She hated tracking the budget. She studied the spreadsheet she'd just created on her laptop computer until the numbers blurred. It just would not come out right. She'd underestimated the costs of the building supplies, especially because of the extra plumbing—Max had been right about that—and even with the great deal she'd gotten on arty black chairs and faux granite tables, whenever she hit the "total," the program threw error symbols.

She sighed and looked up. Just beyond her laptop Max was bent over, hammering the planks of the stage steps. He had such a great butt. She sighed in frustration. Max had stayed physically distant from her for the entire week and begged off whenever she invited him to dinner. Of course, the diet dinner she'd nuked for him the night they went over her plans hadn't exactly been gourmet, but she doubted her cooking was the problem.

He braced a plank with his hip, then put the nail in

place, preparing to hammer it in. He was the sexiest handyman she'd ever seen. She shifted slightly so she wouldn't be distracted by the sight of those muscular arms, those thick thighs, that butt....

"Ow!" Max exclaimed. He dropped the hammer and grabbed the hand he must have smashed with it. He might be the sexiest handyman she'd ever seen, but he was certainly not the most skilled.

"I'll get some ice!" Lacey said. She rushed to the ice chest and scooped cubes into a plastic cup, which she carried to him.

"I'm fine," he said through gritted teeth.

"It'll keep the swelling down," she said, pushing the cup at him.

Reluctantly, Max stuck his smashed forefinger and thumb into the ice and took the cup from her. "Thanks."

She looked past him, tilted her head and closed one eye to study the plank he'd hammered. "That step's crooked."

Max turned to check it out. "It is not."

"Yes, it is." She went to the stage, picked up the level and set it on the step. The bubble was way over the line.

"Damn," Max said.

"No biggie. It's a mistake anyone could make," she said, hoping she hadn't bruised his ego. Not likely. Max was so masculine, so sure of himself, she doubted her criticism would have any effect on him. Thank goodness the three assistants she'd hired knew their way around a circular saw. Max McLane's rapid calculations on the Quonset hut art studio had led her to the wrong conclusions about his construction competence. Of course, her judgment probably had been colored by how much she wanted to sleep with him. Not a good basis for a hiring decision, that was for sure. And she'd thought she was really good at hiring.

She picked up the hammer, braced her foot on the wood and pried out the nail with a satisfying squeak. She really loved the chance to get her hands dirty. Rodney, one of the assistants, had showed her how to use the saws and she'd cut most of the boards for the frame for the liquor bar. Rodney'd actually said she had a good eye. High praise from the taciturn worker.

In a few seconds, she'd hammered the step straight. When she turned back around, she saw that Max was studying her computer.

"You've got the wrong factor here for per-piece costs," he said.

"Really?" She walked over to look over his shoulder. His short hair revealed the nice curve of his skull and his great ears. She liked the muscular line of his neck as it disappeared into the open collar of his brown cotton shirt. Straight, dark hair poked up from his chest at the vee of his shirt. She thought about how his bare chest had looked when he'd stripped to wash off the car oil. No tattoo, but everything else she could ever want. She wondered how he looked below the waist. She shivered. "How did you get to know so much about spreadsheets?" She'd let her fantasy color her words, she could tell by the tone he took when he answered.

"I told you I'm good. At math." He might as well

have said *at sex*. He stood and pulled back the chair. "Sit and I'll show you."

She sat and he reached past her cheek to point at the screen with a forefinger that wore a bandage. He'd sliced it with a mat knife. His sleeve brushed her bare arm, giving her goose bumps. "See the sum here?"

"Yes," she said, but she felt like she was in his arms. She could feel his heat, smell the nice musk of his skin and aftershave, sense his breath going in and out.

"That sum doesn't reflect..." His words faded. "It doesn't reflect..."

She glanced up and saw he was staring down at her breasts. Feminine satisfaction rushed through her. She shifted so her cleavage deepened. "It doesn't reflect what?" she asked innocently.

"The sum of this column," he said in a rush. She could see red underneath his tan and a haze of lust in his eyes.

Before things could go further, they heard a yelp from the kitchen, some cursing in Spanish and the sound of rushing water.

"Omigod!" She leapt to her feet and raced to the kitchen, where water geysered from the back of the sink. Ramón held the faucet, which had obviously broken off.

"I can *not* work under these conditions," Ramón said. He handed the faucet to Lacey and stomped off. "Plus I need a better fryer," he called over his shoulder as he left.

Max put a stewpot upside-down over the fountain of water and dived under the sink for the shut-off valve.

Lacey ran to get tools from the stage area. She snagged a pair of pliers, a crescent wrench and a sledgehammer for good measure. By the time she got back, Max had succeeded in turning off the water. He sat on the floor soaked to his waist and looked up at her.

He nodded at her armload of tools. "Your confidence in me is stunning."

"Just being prepared."

Max climbed to his feet until he stood tall before her and close. Very close. "That was refreshing," he said, shaking water from his hair. Drops sprinkled onto her own wet face.

"You're all wet." She took in his handsome, water-kissed features. His cheeks gleamed with water and his shirt clung to his muscles.

"You, too." His gaze dipped to Lacey's chest. "Black lace," he murmured. "Nice."

Ye gods, he could see through her wet blouse to her bra beneath. He reached out to coil a damp curl of her hair around one finger. "Curly when wet."

Wet. A little thrill went through her at the way he said the word. Like *wet* every place she could be wet.

In the silence, they heard water drip from the ceiling and appliances. *Plip, plip, plip.*

Max groaned and closed his eyes. When he opened them they were dark with heat. "You tempt me, Lacey," he said, his voice thick with longing, "too much."

"Just give in," she whispered. "We both want it."

"Lacey..." His hands cupped her face, his thumb gently brushed her lip. He looked as though the sensation caused him pain. He wanted her and she loved it.

"We've been through this before. This would be just sex, Lacey. Nothing more."

"That's what I want."

He shook his head like he knew her better than she knew herself. "When did you ever have just sex?"

"Lots of times," she lied. It was uncanny the way he seemed to know her. It was true that sex had always been part of a relationship for her. But that was the whole problem. She didn't know sex's possibilities and she wanted him to teach her.

"Lacey," he chided. "I'll bet money you have a boyfriend right now, don't you?"

"Not anymore," she said, jutting her chin at him. "I broke up with him. And what I want now is sex, pure and simple." She leaned closer, within kissing range.

"Sex is never simple," Max said slowly.

"Yes, it is. It's as simple...as...this." She reached up and kissed him. To her delight, after only a second of hesitation, he kissed her back, long and sweet and hard. Just when her knees were about to buckle, he broke it off. "I've got to take care of the plumbing," he whispered.

"I know," she said, dazed. She opened her eyes and he was gone. When she heard him tell Rodney he was going to the Home Depot store, she realized, of course, that the plumbing he meant was of the kitchen variety.

LACEY TOSSED and turned all night, thinking about Max and trying to keep from rolling into the wall. She *had* to get this bed fixed. She'd ask Rodney in the morning. He was a wonder with metal. Unlike Max, who didn't know a jigsaw from a circular saw. Maybe she'd help and Rodney could teach her to weld. So far, she'd had good luck with wood and plaster—she'd helped frame the new window and plaster the arch between the new section and the old—but metal was a different challenge.

That settled, what was she going to do about Max? He thought she'd take sex too seriously. How could she convince him she could be as easygoing about it as he could? The only thing she could think of was having a fling with someone else. Except she didn't want anyone else. Just Max.

That didn't mean she wanted to get *serious* or anything. She just happened to be attracted to only one man at a time. So how could she convince Max they could do it with no strings attached?

She slugged her pillow and rolled over to try and sleep, except she slid into the wall. Damn. She'd definitely get Rodney to fix this thing tomorrow.

The next afternoon, Lacey showed Rodney the broken bed and he set to work hammering the frame back into shape while she studied his technique for future reference. He was a cute guy, she realized. Midtwenties. Easygoing. Capable. And thoughtful. Maybe she could sleep with him? He was a little young for her, but if she could manage it, a little bouncy-bouncy with Rodney and she could prove to Max she could be casual about the big "I."

"I think that'll hold, Ms. Lacey," Rodney said, standing up and coming toward her. "The joint may be a little weak now, but I reinforced it some. To weld it, I'd have to bring it outside."

"Let's go with this for now."

"If you want, I can show you how to weld when we change the pipes in the kitchen."

"Sounds great." She looked him over. *So, how about a little horizontal mambo with Rodney?* But she couldn't do it. She didn't feel anything. No spark, no chemistry, no flash of heat like she felt with Max. Too bad. "Thanks, then."

"No prob, Ms. Lacey."

Lacey glanced past his shoulder through the screen of her open window and saw that Max was heading their way. He probably needed the keys to the truck.

And that gave her an idea. She didn't have to actually *have* a fling, she just had to make Max believe she'd had one.

Abruptly, she flopped onto the bed. "I just want to try it out," she explained to Rodney, pausing for a second to give Max time to reach the trailer. Then she said, "Ooooh, this feels soo goood," breathily, but loud. She rolled around on the mattress then bounced hard. "Mmm. You are sooo good at what you do."

"Thanks," Rodney said, looking at her like she was crazy. "It was just a bent leg. No big deal."

"No, I mean it. You are wonnn-derful. This feels sooo good." Surely, Max had heard that.

Rodney backed toward the door, his face red.

"Don't go," she said, leaping off the bed. "Wait here and I'll pay you."

"That's okay. We can settle up later." He looked a little scared.

"Why don't you...um...check the closet. The right panel is about to come off its rail," she said, getting between him and the bedroom door.

"Okay," he said nervously.

She closed Rodney in the bedroom just as Max knocked at the front door. As she hurried across the living room, she whipped off her blouse and bra, tousled her hair, pinched her lips, then held the shirt up to her chin. She opened the door slightly and leaned in the opening, hoping she looked like a woman who'd been interrupted midboff. "Max! What brings you here?"

He stared at her, looking exactly as she'd hoped—jealous and stimulated and pink under his tan. "I need Jasper's truck keys," he said slowly, a little puzzled. "Looks like I caught you at a bad time."

She tossed her hair back. "Actually, I *am* a little *busy*." She winked at him. "I do that now and then, you know. Get *busy*."

Abruptly, he grinned and his eyes twinkled. "You don't say," he drawled.

"I swear I didn't touch her, Mr. McLane," Rodney said behind her. Damn.

Lacey jerked around, clutching her blouse against her chest and found Rodney holding up his hands as if Max might have a gun.

"I just fixed the bed. That's all. She flipped out on me and started bouncing on the bed saying weird stuff."

Max could barely restrain his laughter, she saw, and his eyes twinkled merrily.

"It was just a joke, Rodney," Lacey said. "I can explain—"

"That's okay. I gotta go," Rodney said, easing past her and out the door.

"I have to pay you," she called to him.

"No need," he called back, practically running.

"Considering how excited you got about a bed repair, I can't wait to see what you'll do when we finish the stage," Max drawled. "We'll have to put a wallet between your teeth so you don't swallow your tongue."

"Very funny!" she said, embarrassed, irritated and, to tell the truth, amused, too. She shut the door in his face.

Max knocked at the door. She pulled her shirt over her head and opened the door. "What?" she demanded.

"The keys?"

"Oh." She stomped to her purse, fished out the keys and brought them to him. "Here!"

"Don't be mad. It was cute, okay? I'm flattered." His brown eyes searched her face.

"I just wanted to show you that sex isn't that big a deal to me."

"Even if that's true, Lacey, you don't really know me or who I am or—"

"Sure I do. You're a man and I'm a woman. That's all I need to know."

"It's not that simple. Our lives are entirely different. We live in very different worlds."

"I know. I like how different you are."

"You don't know the half of it," he said, with a wry

smile. He bounced the keys in his hand, tugged his Stetson hat in farewell and walked away with that great swagger, leaving Lacey pondering his last excuse for not sleeping with her: *We live in very different worlds.*

Okay, time to make their worlds collide.

6

SHE LOOKED just like she'd stepped off a billboard for Lady Wrangler jeans, Lacey thought, evaluating herself as best she could in the mirror in the trailer's cramped bathroom. She wore her tightest jeans, along with her used-clothing store steals—a ruffled, pearl-snap rodeo blouse in virginal white, red cowboy boots and a matching Stetson hat.

If the problem was that she and Max were from different worlds, then she'd just mosey over to his for a while. She'd started that at the cowboy bar, but she'd ruined it by getting drunk. Now she had to show Max she was really into the cowboy thing.

Her plan was to ask Max to take her on a horseback tour of the ranch. She hadn't been on a horse since she was a kid, but it had to be like riding a bike—you never forgot. Today was a perfect day since they had to let the saltillo tile set and couldn't work on the coffeehouse.

She'd briefly considered dropping the idea of sleeping with Max, but it had become a challenge, a test of the new Lacey—the woman who set goals and went after them. Maybe a fling wasn't a fabulous goal, but it was a compelling one. Because of Max. Something about him—his cowboyness, of course, but more than that, his complexity, his intelligence—drew her in, made her want more. She couldn't get him out of her thoughts or her dreams. He'd practically become an obsession. She knew they'd be great together, just as she knew she'd be great for Wellington Restaurant Corp.

It also gave her a place to expend her nervous energy, and something else to think about besides the coffeehouse, which she tended to agonize over. Why shouldn't she have it all?

Max was holding back, but it was just a matter of chivalry. That was charming, but enough already.

This ought to meet his last objection. She'd be smack-dab in the middle of his world and she'd love it, she was sure. Max's passion for ranching would rub off on her. Her passion for him would rub off on him. And soon they'd be rubbing their passions together like flint and steel in tinder.

She snugged the hat on her head at a determined angle and strode across the highway, feeling sexy, tough and wild in her cowgirl outfit. She found Max in the barn, walking a horse into its stall.

"If you'd pick up the pace, I could get you back here for your afternoon snack a hell of a lot faster," he told the animal.

"Hey, there, pardner," Lacey drawled, one hand to her hat, propping a foot on a hay bale, acting out the Wrangler jeans ad.

Max stared at her. "What are you doing here?" He paused. "Looking like *that*." He liked it. Goodie.

"I was hoping you'd take me on a horseback ride around the Rockin' W."

"Why would I do that?" He pushed his hat back with his thumb.

"It'd be fun. We can't work on the coffeehouse anyway. And I like riding." She paused. "I *love* it, actually."

He shook his head, grinning. "You never give up, do you?" He removed the horse's saddle and blanket and patted her flank, raising dust.

"Come on, Max. It'll be fun." She hurried closer to him. "You can show me everything about the ranch—what you love, how it works, everything."

Yeah, right, Max thought. A former accountant was supposed to show her how the ranch worked. Hell, he barely knew how his horse worked.

"Like, for example, what's this for?" Lacey asked, holding up a long looped piece of leather. He had no clue what it was. But he couldn't let her know that. "Uh, that's a bridle deal."

"Deal? That a technical term?"

"Never mind. Are you sure you want to do this?"

"Absolutely. Which horse should I ride?"

Oh, God. He couldn't think of a reason to turn her down. At least on horseback, she'd be out of kissing range. "You ever been on a horse before?" he asked.

"Not since I was a kid. But I loved it then. A lot."

"It's not as easy as it looks," he said. "You have to show the horse you're the boss and move with confidence."

"Maybe you can demonstrate for me."

"Right," he said. It was an even bet he'd end up on his ass when he climbed onto any horse but Seesaw.

He started to bridle Seesaw, but the horse gave him

that *look*. She expected to kick back and take a snooze, or whatever horses did when they weren't working—shoo flies and compare notes with the other horses, he guessed.

So, he chose a brown gelding that looked as laid-back as Seesaw. He picked out the right-size bridle and the horse only snorted a little when he put it on and led him out into the yard. Max managed to get the saddle on and cinched down with a minimum of jerking and dodging by the horse. So far so good for his cowboy cover.

Now, to get Lacey on board.

"Can you climb on okay?" he asked her.

"It's been a while." She bit her lip nervously. God, that got to him.

"Okay. Step on," he said. He formed a stirrup with his hands.

She placed a boot-clad foot there, rested one small hand on his shoulder, reached up for the saddle horn with the other, and hopped up. And then back down. "These jeans are a little tight," she said breathlessly.

She leaned more fully against him—could she be pressing her breasts against him on purpose? If so, God bless her. She dug her fingers into his shoulder, wobbling as she tried to stretch her leg over the horse's back. No luck.

"Allow me," he said, and he put his hands around her narrow waist, steeling himself against how great it felt to hold her like that. He swung her high enough to get her leg over the horse's back and then she dropped into the saddle. Her eyes caught his and he felt that zing from their green depths.

She looked natural on a horse. The rodeo queen blouse was very feminine, the hat put a mysterious shadow on her face and her hair spilled out in pretty waves that gleamed in the sun.

She sat tall in the saddle, a position that emphasized how round and firm her behind was. The saddle horn nestled right against the vee of her legs. Right *there*.

His body declared how much he appreciated the sight. "You might want to scoot back a little," he said, as much for his peace of mind as for her stability. He wanted to yank her off that horse and into his arms and kiss that puffy mouth until it bruised.

As if reading his mind, her horse swung its head and whapped Max so hard he took a step backward. Whoever said horses were dumb?

Now *he* needed a horse. Back in the stable, he did a quick *eeny-meeny-miny-mo* and settled on a red-brown horse a little taller than Seesaw, who looked nice.

With hardly any trouble, he slipped a bridle on and slid the bit in the horse's mouth. It only required a minor adjustment and a modest tug-of-war to get him out of the stable. Max looped the reins around the fence post and went for a saddle, but when he got back, his horse seemed to be picking a fight with Lacey's, nosing it and whinnying.

Lacey's horse jerked to the side. Lacey yelped.

"Hang on," he said, yanking his horse away. "Keep your hips loose and move with the horse." But Lacey didn't need any advice about how to move those hips.

We'd like to send you **2 FREE** books and a surprise gift to introduce you to Harlequin Temptation®. Accept our special offer today and

Indulge in a Harlequin Moment!

HOW TO QUALIFY:

1. With a coin, carefully scratch off the silver area on the card at right to see what we have for you—**2 FREE BOOKS** and a **FREE GIFT**—**ALL YOURS! ALL FREE!**

2. Send back the card and you'll receive two brand-new Harlequin Temptation® books. These books have a cover price of $3.99 each in the U.S. and $4.50 each in Canada, but they are yours to keep absolutely free!

3. There's no catch. You're under no obligation to buy anything. We charge nothing—ZERO—for your first shipment and you don't have to make any minimum number of purchases—not even one!

4. The fact is, thousands of readers enjoy receiving books by mail from the Harlequin Reader Service®. They enjoy the convenience of home delivery... they like getting the best new novels at discount prices, BEFORE they're available in stores...and they love their *Heart to Heart* subscriber newsletter featuring author news, horoscopes, recipes, book reviews and much more!

5. We hope that after receiving your free books you'll want to remain a subscriber. But the choice is yours—to continue or cancel, any time at all. So why not take us up on our invitation with no risk of any kind. You'll be glad you did!

SPECIAL FREE GIFT!

We can't tell you what it is...but we're sure you'll like it! A FREE gift just for giving the Harlequin Reader Service® a try!

Visit us online at
www.eHarlequin.com

The **2 FREE BOOKS** we send you will be selected from **HARLEQUIN TEMPTATION**®, the series that brings you sexy, sizzling and seductive stories.

Books received may vary.

Scratch off the silver area to see what the Harlequin Reader Service has for you.

HARLEQUIN®
Makes any time special™

YES! I have scratched off the silver area above. Please send me the **2 FREE** books and gift for which I qualify. I understand I am under no obligation to purchase any books, as explained on the back and on the opposite page.

342 HDL DH4W   142 HDL DH4V

FIRST NAME	LAST NAME

ADDRESS

APT.#	CITY

STATE/PROV.	ZIP/POSTAL CODE

Offer limited to one per household and not valid to current Harlequin Temptation® subscribers. All orders subject to approval.

THE HARLEQUIN READER SERVICE® — Here's how it works:

Accepting your 2 free books and gift places you under no obligation to buy anything. You may keep the books and gift and return the shipping statement marked "cancel." If you do not cancel, about a month later we'll send you 4 additional books and bill you just $3.34 each in the U.S., or $3.80 each in Canada, plus 25¢ shipping & handling per book and applicable tax, if any.* That's the complete price and — compared to cover prices of $3.99 each in the U.S. and $4.50 each in Canada — it's quite a bargain! You may cancel at any time, but if you choose to continue, every month we'll send you 4 more books, which you may either purchase at the discount price or return to us and cancel your subscription.

*Terms and prices subject to change without notice. Sales tax applicable in N.Y. Canadian residents will be charged applicable provincial taxes and GST.

She rocked nicely in that smooth leather saddle. Mmm, he sure would like some of that action.

When he went to saddle his horse, he saw the reins had slipped off the fence, so the creature was loose. It decided to play tag, so he ended up chasing it around the paddock with the saddle until it stopped to snuffle the business end of Lacey's horse. At that point, he slapped on the saddle, did a quick cinch job and climbed aboard.

"Don't you want that more snug?" Lacey asked, indicating his saddle.

"It's fine," he said. "Let's get going."

"What are you up to there, McLane?" Buck drawled from the fence. "Howdy, Miss Lacey." He tilted his hat at her.

"Hi, Buck," she said.

"What brings you to the Rockin' W? I haven't seen you around here since you were little."

"Max is going to take me on a horseback tour of the ranch."

"Oh, is he now?" Buck's leather-brown face creased into a grin.

"Unless you need me around here," Max said eagerly.

"Oh, no. You go on now and have fun." Buck bent to pick up Max's fallen hat and leaned out to hand it to Max, speaking quietly for Max's ears only. "You're riding Starfire. He's a lazy cuss, who likes to scrape riders off under tree branches, so watch yourself."

Max nodded.

"You're in good hands, Miss Lacey," Buck said.

"McLane's one of my best men." Buck winked at Max. He was one of his *only* men. "Be sure and get his ideas on cost-saving and such."

"Oh, I will," Lacey said.

Buck chuckled and shook his head.

"Shall we go?" Lacey asked. She turned her horse and urged it into a trot with an efficient maneuver of her reins.

After a few seconds of wordless struggle, Max managed to get Starfire to do the same at a do-I-*have*-to pace. This was going to be a long afternoon, he could tell already.

AN HOUR LATER, Max lay on the sofa in Lacey's trailer, wearing an ice-filled bag Lacey had insisted on putting on his head.

"It wasn't your fault, Max. I mean the horse was trying to scrape you off. You *had* to shift to the side."

"Yeah, and if I'd tightened the girth after we got out of the gate, the saddle wouldn't have slid," he said. "They always puff out their rib cages when you saddle them."

"Still, it could happen to any cowboy. How's your head?"

"It's fine. It's a small bump, that's all. I don't even need this ice pack."

"Just leave it there. We want to keep the swelling down. You don't feel sleepy, do you? That's a clue that you've had a concussion. Let me look into your eyes."

They were so brown, so deep, she wanted to melt into them. But she forced herself to examine his pupils to see

if they were equally dilated. Dark spots in the middle of brown velvet, they seemed okay—soft yet so intense....
Stop that, Lacey.

"Let me get something for your cheek," she called to him as she headed to the bathroom for some medicine.

"It's just some scrapes," he called back. "Forget it."

Max sure seemed to get hurt a lot around her. He'd banged his hand changing the oil, nearly threw up in the diner, collected not a few handyman wounds and now had fallen off his horse. She hoped she wasn't some kind of jinx for him.

She hurried back into the living room with her supplies and sat next to him, her knees brushing his sides pleasantly. At least nursing him gave her a legitimate reason to get so close.

"I had a great time on the ranch," she said, dipping a swab into the peroxide. "I can see why you like working outdoors. Fresh air, exercise, working with the cattle. You did a good job fixing that fence post."

"You said it was crooked." He smirked at her.

"Just a tad. And then, you got that calf out of that rock crevice. That was so great." She dabbed the scrapes on both cheeks with the swab.

"You're killing me, Lacy," Max said.

"It's just a little peroxide, for crying out loud."

"I don't mean that," he said huskily, taking the hand with the cotton swab in both of his work-roughened ones. His eyes locked with hers.

Warmth shot from her fingers down to her toes. "Oh. I see." Boy, did she. At last here was the part of the movie where the heroine fixed up the hero, their eyes meet and poof, love scene! Any second they'd be kissing as peroxide fumes and sexual heat rose around them. Her bed was just a few feet away. Or they could stay right here on the sofa. Max was already lying down. She felt like she'd just cranked her way to the top of the first hill on a roller coaster, anticipating the downward whoosh and thrill. *Here we go....*

Before she could even moisten her lips, Max sat up and his mouth met hers, hot and strong, even better than after the kitchen sink geyser. She tilted slightly to give him better access to her mouth. His kiss felt so good, so right. Like magic. Their tongues had finally touched and it was hot heaven when ice-cold plastic suddenly came between them. The ice bag had slid from Max's head to their noses.

They pulled apart and the ice bag fell to Max's lap. Lacey pushed it to the floor. The last place she wanted iced was Max's *lap*. She leaned in to pick up where they'd left off, but Max pulled away. "We can't do this, Lacey." Heat flamed in his dark eyes, contradicting his words. He was practically panting. So was she.

"Sure we can. Why can't we?" She ticked off his previous objections on her fingers. "I'm not drunk. We both agree this is just a casual thing and I just told you how much I enjoy your world. So, what's the problem?" She closed her eyes and leaned in for more kissing.

She felt him hesitate, then he breathed, "Oh, hell," and kissed her, hard and fast. Almost immediately, he yanked himself away. "I've got to go," he said.

"Why?" she said, dazed by the slam-bam kiss.

"I've got stalls to muck."

"Stalls to muck? What?" Her daze evaporated. "You'd rather shovel manure than go to bed with me?"

"That's not it, Lacey." He pinned her with a look, a world of hunger in his eyes. "If I stay here one more minute," he said, his voice raw with need, "I won't be able to leave."

Then he grabbed his hat and headed for the door, where he stopped and turned to her. "See you tomorrow," he said, his eyes lingering on her.

"Yeah," she said faintly, stunned by what he'd just said. "See you tomorrow."

Wow. Max wanted her so much that all it would take would be one more kiss and he wouldn't be able to stop. One more kiss. *Okay*, she thought, flopping back onto the couch, *I'll take that as a personal challenge.*

"So, how'd the tour go?" Buck asked Max the next morning as they shared coffee in the stable before setting off to check fences, round up stray cattle and distribute salt blocks.

"Fine, I guess." Absently, he rubbed the lump on the top of his head. "I just wish you'd told Lacey that Starfire's name was Widowmaker. Would have saved me some dignity at least."

"You hit the dirt, huh?"

"Oh, yeah."

Buck looked at him speculatively. "I gotta wonder if you know what you're doing, son."

"I didn't recinch him after we got out of the gate."

"No, I mean with Miss Lacey. She's a sweet soul. She'd fall for a smooth line."

"I'm not giving her any lines, Buck. I swear. I'm doing my level best to watch out for her without, uh..."

"Thinking with your privates? Good. I know you'll do the right thing. Wade'd mow flat anyone that took advantage of his sister. Maybe stick to cold showers, son."

"Or ice bags."

"Beg your pardon?"

"Nothing." The ice bag had saved him yesterday in the trailer. Despite his best efforts, he kept ending up in kissing range of Lacey. He'd have to stay out of that tiny trailer and its convenient bed.

The worst of it was that if even Buck suspected something was going on, then it must be as obvious as the bowling-ball-size cherry on the top of Jasper's six-foot ice-cream-cone sculpture.

Buck studied him thoughtfully. "You know, Ray, from over the Red Arroyo Ranch, could pitch in around here," he finally said. "How about if you work over at the café full-time for a while. That way you can get in, get the job done and get out. Less temptation."

Max watched Buck's face. He did not want to let the man down. "That would probably be good, Buck. If you're sure you don't need me."

"We'll be fine."

"Then I'll take you up on your offer. Anyway, I know I haven't been much help to you around here."

"You did fine," Buck said affectionately. "You remind me of my son. He belonged in the city, too." He paused, bent to spit some tobacco into the dirt, then gave Max a speculative look. "You know, you might be able to help a friend of mine."

"How's that?"

"Riley Stoker's got a way with leather. And he's made up these everyday halters that don't cost much. They'd be real popular at riding stables and such, but he's got no head for figures. He needs someone to show him how to sell 'em. Would you sit down with him and look over what he's got?"

"I'd be glad to."

"Great," Buck said. "Now, why don't you load the salt blocks into the truck?"

Max headed off, grateful Buck had suggested a way to lessen the time he spent around Lacey.

Why the hell did he act like a teenager in the first rush of hormones around her? Even if she wasn't Wade's sister and he didn't have the job of supervising her, Lacey Wellington was not his type.

They were worlds apart, though not the way Lacey thought. Like Heather, his rich girlfriend from college, Lacey'd grown up with money and the unconscious security that went with it. Her family's wealth was a safety net for any financial tightrope she might walk. Max, on the other hand, succeeded or failed on his own. No one was there to pick him up and dust him off if he fell—though Lacey had been doing a lot of that lately with her trusty peroxide swabs. He could accept that— he almost liked it—but he'd never accept any financial first aid from her, or anyone else, for that matter.

He liked being self-sufficient and he wanted a

woman who understood that and valued it. Lacey didn't act like money mattered to her, but Max knew it made a difference. It showed in the way she was chasing that crazy corporate dream.

Lacey was not the kind of woman he wanted, so he was at a loss to explain the intensity of his attraction to her—the way she stopped his heart, then started it again like electric paddles.

Besides, according to Wade, she was almost engaged. And, even if she had broken up with the guy, like she'd said, Lacey was not the fling type. Those green eyes were determined and independent, but they were also vulnerable. She could be hurt, and hurt bad. Max didn't want to hurt her. Nor would he allow anyone else to. For a moment, he wanted to check out this Pierce guy and see if he was good enough for Lacey. Something angry and heavy filled his chest at the thought of that corporate candy ass with his hands on Lacey.

On second thought, maybe it would be better if he never set eyes on the guy. He might go cowboy and coldcock him on sight. God, all this Wild West stuff was getting to him. Just the same, if he caught wind of this Pierce jerk bothering Lacey *in any way*, there'd be a showdown at the Not-So-OK Corral.

7

"LACEY, I THINK it's time we talked."

Uh-oh. It was Pierce on the phone. She hadn't heard from him since they'd broken up and she'd hoped that meant he'd accepted her decision.

"You've had three weeks to think things through and now I need to see you."

Obviously, he hadn't.

Lacey uprighted the stool she'd been stapling zebra-striped fabric onto and sat on it. "Nothing's changed, Pierce."

"Give me a chance to talk to you. There's a reception for the California guys on Friday. We can talk, then I'll take you out to Alberto's for Flaming Flan Fantastique." He paused. "Your favorite."

"I can't, Pierce. I'm busy here."

"You can take one evening off, can't you?"

"Not this Friday." In fact, she was auditioning bands for the grand opening, but she couldn't tell him that. He might tell Wade her plan and ruin everything.

"Come up here, Lace. I miss you. We're just suffering the strain of being apart."

"I'm sorry you miss me, Pierce, but it's for the best. I—"

"Come and taste this," Ramón shouted from the kitchen. "Now!"

"There's a problem in the kitchen, Pierce. I've got to run. I'll call you back." She hung up, wondering what more she could say.

The problem in the kitchen was that Ramón had gotten as temperamental and demanding as a famous chef, expecting her to drop everything and run to taste a new sauce, salsa or pastry. It would have been irritating if it hadn't been so cute, and the food hadn't been so good.

She headed to the kitchen, worrying as she went. She wasn't sorry to miss an awkward encounter with Pierce, but she wished she could be at the reception for the California guys. She felt a surge of envy that she hadn't been in on the negotiations for the California properties. She was out of the loop down here in this little way station. She'd gotten so carried away with the renovation, her long-term goal had slipped into the background. She should have been talking with Wade about the California plans, e-mailing him her ideas.

Oh, well. In six weeks, once she'd succeeded with the Wonder Coffeehouse, she'd have proven herself to Wade and she'd be where she wanted to be—in the middle of all the corporate doings she could want. She'd be up to her neck in flaming flan.

When she walked through the archway headed for the kitchen, she noticed Max at a booth with a weathered-looking cowboy. Both were huddled over her laptop, and Max was explaining something to the guy, who nodded. Next to the computer was a pile of what looked like bridles.

What the heck were cowboys doing with a computer? She guessed she didn't know much about modern ranching. Of course they had to figure acreage and feed costs, but still, she'd been surprised at how well Max had taken to her budget.

At that moment, the cowboy shook Max's hand, thanked him, gathered up his bridles and left.

Max looked up and caught her eye. He carried the laptop to where she stood by the counter, and set it down next to a bunch of papers he'd been working on.

"What was that all about?" she asked him.

"That was a friend of Buck's. I was just giving him a little help with...um, some math," he said, sounding uncomfortable. He picked up a pencil and tapped it on a paper. It was a very sharp pencil. Kind of anal for a cowboy, but then what did she know? The more she knew about Max, she realized, the less she knew about cowboys.

He had sawdust in his hair and he looked adorably mussed, too. She realized she'd rather have Max McLane in a pile of hay in the barn on Friday night than all the flaming flan in the world. Best of all would be to have Max *and* flaming flan.

"About time," Ramón said, catching sight of her through the pass-through. "Taste this." He handed out a ladle full of a dark brown gravy. "Mole," he said.

She sipped the warm liquid. It was spicy chocolate, buttery and rich. Perfect. "Mmm," she said. She looked up to catch Max's eyes on her.

"Want a taste?" she asked him. She held her hand under the brimming ladle, careful not to spill, and moved it closer. Max's lips parted, ready to accept what she offered and their eyes locked. The moment froze in time, warm and intimate. Lacey's insides sizzled. Max's eyes were as dark as the chili-chocolate sauce she held out to him, and she felt like she might dissolve like the sauce on his tongue.

Still staring at her, Max sipped the sauce. "Mmm," he said, meaning what he was looking at as much as what he was tasting, she could tell. Then he closed his eyes with the pleasure of it. Would he do that during sex? Would he consider her delicious?

"*Diós mío*," Ramón muttered. "Getta room."

Lacey blushed and she could swear Max did, too. "That tastes fabulous, Ramón," she said in as normal a voice as she could manage, handing the ladle back. "Definitely add that to the menu."

"Ramón's some chef," Max said to her in an ordinary voice, clearly trying to change the subject.

"The best. He's even got the temperament." She couldn't catch Max's eye. He'd been stubbornly distant since the ice-bag incident. All she needed was one more kiss and she'd have him, but she wasn't about to attack him. The timing had to be right.

"I ordered the sound system we talked about," he said.

"Can we afford it?" Anxiety pinged inside her.

"I got a great deal on some refurbished equipment."

"Maybe you should walk me through the budget."

"I tried to a week ago, but you were working on the stage arch."

"I know," she said. "I shouldn't be so hands-on." It

was just so fun watching the way the wood fit in place as they'd planned when they'd cut it.

"You're a wonder with a buzz saw, Lacey." His smile teased her.

"I guess so." She frowned. She'd probably gotten too caught up in the building process, leaving the budget in Max's hands. On the other hand, he seemed happier with a spreadsheet than a power sander.

"The budget's fine," he said. *Don't you trust me?* was the question in his eyes.

She trusted him, but maybe she'd depended on him too much. This was her project and her career hung on its success. "I think I need to get up to speed on where we are," she said firmly. "The dollars and cents of it all."

"Okay. Whatever you want. Jasper wants to talk to you about something in his studio. Why don't you go check on that and while you're gone, I'll pull something together?" He sounded weary.

"Okay," she said, doubt nibbling at her. Why was he so reluctant? Was there bad news?

THE STUDIO was starting to take shape, Lacey saw, when she walked through the wooden door into the huge hut—a giant semicircular tunnel of corrugated metal. Jasper had set up his old sculptures at the front end and his equipment and workbenches were at the back of the space, which echoed like an airplane hangar.

The sound of pounding on metal led her to Jasper, who was banging away on the underside of a giant bullfrog made from a kettledrum and assorted pieces of metal.

It was a little too warm, though, she thought, for the hot work he was doing. She'd have to get a couple more cooling units. *Ka-ching*.

"You've done a lot, Jasper," she yelled over the pounding.

Jasper slid out from under the bullfrog and sat up. Sweat rolled down his temples and dripped from his nose. "Hey, girl!"

"The place looks great," she said. Looking at his heat-red face she decided to get the units in ASAP.

"Getting there," he said, grinning from ear to ear. "I'm thinking skylights would help—bring in more light, give a more open feeling. What do you think?"

"Skylights?" *Double ka-ching*. "We could look into that, I guess—once I check the budget. I want to get more cooling for sure."

Jasper whipped a yellow paper from his overall pocket and handed it to her. "Here's the estimate," he said.

"Oh." She studied the paper. Ouch. Then her eye caught scrawled words in the instructions portion of the paper. She looked up at Jasper. "They're coming tomorrow?"

"I can call and cancel if you think it's too much."

"No. It's a great idea," she said weakly. She paused and looked around. There was already an impressive amount of sculpture in the space. "Actually, you'll have this place filled up in no time," she said, turning back to him.

He shrugged. "It's nice to be able to stretch out. I've got that Gremlin chassis coming next week. Can't wait to start building on that. I'm thinking prehistoric turtle."

She looked around again, more deliberately this time, as an idea began to take shape in her mind. "You know, Jasper, you've practically got a whole show here."

"Funny you would say that," Jasper said, a flicker of interest in his eyes. "One of my old art co-op buds was out here yesterday to see what I'm doing. He had the owner of the Art To Go Gallery with him. The guy said he'd had some people asking for work from me. It could have been B.S., though."

"I bet not. The city of Tucson doesn't commission work from nobodies. You're practically an icon, Uncle Jasper. I bet you have a following you don't even know about."

"You're not exactly objective, Lacey. You're my biggest fan." He looked at her with affection. "Though a show might be fun...."

"A show, yes, but I'm getting an even better idea." She paused, as the picture formed in her mind. "Why don't we turn this place into a gallery?"

"A gallery? Nah, that's too complicated. I'm no business guy."

"You hire people for the business end, Jasper. You're the *artist*." She surveyed the space, imagining a crowd of patrons admiring his barbed wire Eiffel Tower and giant ice-cream cone, wandering from his kettledrum bullfrog to the appliance totem pole.

It would be fabulous. She began to walk forward,

talking as she moved. "We could partition off the studio area—use some glass refrigerator blocks maybe... Create a dropped ceiling so you could suspend lighter pieces overhead." She took a few steps forward. "We'd build the reception desk up front. Leave the curved walls, but use sheetrock to attach wall sculptures. It would still have an industrial look, but with the Jasper Wellington whimsy."

The vision complete, she turned on her heels to face him. "We could do it. It would take a couple months to build. And, of course you'd have to renew your contacts in the art community, get some buzz going. Heck, you could host other artists, too. What do you think?"

"I don't know, Lacey." He shook his head. "I'm having fun now. That's enough."

"Don't sell yourself short, Jasper. This could be great. It's the obvious next step."

"Honey, you just worry about the café," Jasper said. "I'm cookin' with gas right now. Everything's hunky-dory. Well, when the skylights are put in. And maybe some track lighting...and some spots."

Somehow, she knew Jasper's "hunky-dory" would cost a chunk of change. On the other hand, if the studio became a gallery, she might be able to get a business loan and roll the skylights and AC and other enhancements into the loan. "I'll talk to Max about the budget," she said.

"I'm really fine," he said. "Really. Once we get a new lathe in here, of course...."

She hoped desperately Max hadn't been hiding bad financial news from her, because she'd just discovered a fabulous new investment that, knowing Jasper, would get pricier by the minute.

WHEN MAX RAN through the spreadsheet with her an hour later, Lacey was delighted to find the budget looked fat. "I was sure we'd overspent," she said to him, handing him a plate of warmed-up tamale experiments Ramón had left for them to sample. She sat on the counter stool beside him and took a swallow from one of the long-necked Tecates beers she'd fetched for them.

"It worked out," Max said, shrugging. "You just didn't realize all the, uh, resources you had."

"Maybe not." She frowned. She could have sworn the advertising budget he'd shown her was bigger than before. And weren't some costs missing? She wished she'd tracked things more closely.

"I don't know how you did it," she said slowly. Could Max have made a mistake? She made a mental note to check her earlier cost projections.

"Like I said, it's a numbers thing."

"I guess so." No. *Have a little faith.* Max was her employee and he'd just done what she'd assigned him to do. "Well, you're just a wonder with numbers, that's all I can say."

"It wasn't anything. I mean it." He acted like he'd done something wrong—cheated her—instead of having performed a budgetary miracle.

"Seriously, Max. Don't be so modest."

"Believe me, I'm not."

"You know, with your skills, you could be a bookkeeper in a heartbeat. I can give a great recommendation, if you wanted a job in—"

"No, thanks," he said.

"I mean it. You could easily handle—"

"I don't want that kind of work, Lacey," he said, cutting her off, his teeth gritted. "I have no interest in business crap."

"Oh, I'm sorry," she said. His fierceness startled her. "Of course, you're doing what you want to do. I didn't mean to imply that being a cowboy wasn't great or anything. I—"

"Forget it. It was a few calculations." He gave her a tight smile. "No big deal."

"Sure. I guess I just got excited that we're financially solid because I've got a plan for Jasper's place." Her enthusiasm for the project instantly returned, stronger than before now that Max had relieved her budget worries.

"*You've* got a plan? From what I've seen, Jasper has more plans than anyone needs." His earlier tension became amusement.

"He wants to put some skylights in the studio and he needs more cooling units. But I was looking at all the sculpture he's already got and realized we could easily turn the place into a gallery."

"A gallery?"

"Yes. He's been out of circulation for a couple of years, but he used to have regular shows in the downtown galleries—in Phoenix, too. At the University of Arizona and Arizona State, even once at the airport. He mentioned that people still ask about his work. This would really give him a boost. He loves his sculpture so much."

"Interesting..." Max said, watching her closely, his eyes a little glazed.

"It's a great idea, I think. And it'll give Jasper a new lease on life. I've been thinking that he might have been depressed since his leg-break three years ago. And, here's where you can help, Max. I was thinking we could apply for a business loan to reduce our capital outlay. Also, I was thinking that the Arizona Commission on the Arts might be able to help with a grant or something, especially if he started teaching more aspiring disadvantaged kids like Ramón..." She stopped rattling on and looked at him, "So, what do you think? Max?"

Max looked peculiar. His eyes were lit with tenderness and his smile was almost...well, dreamy.

"You're looking at me funny," she said.

"I'm just listening to you, feeling your enthusiasm, that's all."

"Well, cut it out, okay? It's distracting." The last thing she needed when she'd decided to stay in business mode was for Max to look dreamy-eyed at her.

"Sure. No problem." He blinked away the look and composed his face.

"I don't know how I can pull this off when there's so much to do at the coffeehouse." She sighed.

"Really?"

"Oh, yeah. I've got to schedule health and fire inspections and hire waitresses and set up advertising and audition bands."

But as she talked, instead of feeling burdened by the tasks ahead, she felt energized. "There's just a ton of stuff left. Oh, here's an idea. Ramón's sister needs a job. She's into art, so I bet she'd love being the receptionist at Jasper's gallery. Perfect. His younger brothers could use work, too, Ramón says. Maybe they can start out in the kitchen. Helping at first, maybe washing dishes, then work up from there. If they want, I mean. What do you think?"

Max had cupped his chin in his hands and his gaze was locked somewhere around her mouth.

"You're doing it again," she said.

"Doing what?"

"Looking at me that way." She frowned, suspicious. "You're not about to tell me I'm cute, are you?"

"I wouldn't dare," he said, holding up his hands in defense. "I just can't help looking at you. You amaze me."

"I do?" Blush heated her cheeks.

"Yes, you do. You work so hard at this. And you're so...dogged. Indomitable, really. I admire that. And on top of everything, you're helping your uncle."

"I try." His praise went straight to her heart.

"And you'll succeed, too."

"You think so?"

"I know so. And if your brother can't see that, then he's an idiot." His words were fierce, but his expression was tender. He lifted his beer bottle in a toast. "Here's to you, Lacey," he said.

"And to you, Max," she said. "You've done a lot for

me." She clinked her long-neck against his. They both took a swallow.

There was a long silence. Their business was concluded, but neither seemed inclined to leave. Lacey felt the familiar man-woman awareness rise between them, like smoke swirling from an unquenchable fire.

Max cleared his throat. "Anyway, I think we've both done great in controlling our...uh...urges. That would have been a big mistake."

"You really think so?"

"Oh, yeah." He made it sound so final. Like he was completely finished with her. As if sitting so close together on counter stools, their knees nearly touching, had no effect on him at all. Meanwhile, she was practically tingling from the closeness of him. "Here's to self-control," Max said, lifting his bottle for another toast.

Her heart sank. Maybe it *should* be over. How long could she keep trying to seduce him without humiliating herself? It probably was time to give up. "Here's to it," she said on a heavy sigh. What else could she say?

At that moment, her eyes caught movement through the diner window. She watched in horror as a familiar BMW sedan pulled into the parking lot. Pierce. He'd come down here to see her, to talk her into getting back together. Great.

"What's the matter?" Max asked. He started to turn to see what she was looking at.

"N-n-nothing," she said, tugging on his arm so he looked her way. Pierce was getting out of the car. She had to fix this, once and for all. Prove to Pierce she meant what she said. And she knew exactly how to do it. If Max would cooperate...

"Listen, Max. Remember I told you I broke up with my boyfriend? Well, he's coming here right now and I need you to—" Pierce was coming up the porch steps. "Oh, hell." Lacey hopped from her stool onto Max's lap, linked her fingers behind his neck and kissed him firmly.

"Whada yu doon?" he asked, the words garbled against her mouth.

She pulled back long enough to say, "Play along with me, okay? Here he comes." She had to clear all sensible thoughts from Max's head, so she gave him the most lascivious, tongue-wild kiss she could manage, mashing her breasts against his chest, sliding one hand down into the back pocket of his jeans and squeezing his tight butt.

To her immense relief, Max gave a groan, then kissed her back. Really kissed her, holding her against him with the power of a man who could tame a horse or any wild thing he came across. He kissed her thoroughly, achingly, until she felt scalded, practically branded. If Pierce wasn't about to push open that door, she'd let this moment go and go.

The door clanged and Lacey tightened her grip on the back of Max's neck, so he would hold the kiss long enough for Pierce to get the picture.

But Max was having none of that. He reached up and pried her fingers away from his neck and used one booted foot to push their stool to face the man who'd just entered.

"Pierce, what are you doing here?" Lacey asked, acting breathlessly surprised.

"I came to see you." Pierce frowned. "But I seem to have caught you at a bad time." There was a flicker of hurt on his face, which she regretted. She didn't want to rub it in. She just wanted him to believe her.

"This is Max McLane," she said. "And we're together."

She felt Max go tense.

"Max, this is Pierce Winslow, my *ex*-boyfriend."

Max tilted his hat at Pierce and, after a pause, his other arm went protectively around Lacey's waist. Whew! He was going along with her. A good thing, since she hadn't had time to run through his lines with him.

She looked up into Max's face to thank him. The smoke of desire still swirled in his eyes, along with annoyance. He didn't like what she'd done. She'd have to apologize later. Right now, she had to make things clear to Pierce. "I'm sorry you had to see this, but at least now you'll believe that it's over between us."

"Could I speak to you in private?" Pierce asked her.

"We've been through it all before. Anything you have to say to me, you can say in front of Max."

Pierce looked Max over, angry and suspicious. What if he picked a fight with Max? That would be awful! All the squash playing in the world wouldn't give Pierce the strength he'd need to hold his own with a guy who wrestled steers for a living.

Evidently, that fact dawned on him, because he

turned to her. "What are you trying to prove?" Pierce asked fiercely.

"I'm not trying to prove anything."

"Bull—"

"Stop right there, mister." Max was mad as hell that Lacey had dragged him into her little charade, but her fingers dug into his side like she needed him, so he couldn't let her down. Not to mention the fact that the kiss she'd delivered had made his life rush past his eyes. He'd wanted to make love to her on the spot. So, for Lacey's sake, he'd make this dweeb clear out.

"Seems to me the lady here has made her point," Max said in his best Randy-the-Rodeo-Man tone—half growl, half threat. "I believe she'd like you to leave. I expect you to do that. Now."

"Stay out of this," the little jerk said.

The air went cold with tension.

"I am in it," he said levelly. "Lacey and I mean something to each other." Max squeezed Lacey tightly against him. She grinned up at him, triumphant. *Not so fast*, he wanted to warn her. He'd get rid of Pierce, all right, but he planned on teaching her a little lesson afterward.

"Can't you see that Lacey's playing games?" Pierce said.

"She wouldn't do that. You wouldn't play games about anything as serious as the thing between us, would you, darlin'?" he asked her, squeezing her a little too hard.

"Um, no, of course not," she said, then gulped.

"There. Ya see," he said to Pierce. "So, I think you'd

better stop pestering her." Max stood, lifting Lacey to her feet at the same time. He took a step forward. He could take this guy. And, he was annoyed to notice, he kind of wanted to try.

Pierce stood still for just a second while Max gave him a Cowboy Avenger look. Kind of like the look that had sent many a bookkeeper back to revise his figures, except more gritty.

It worked. Pierce stepped backward out of punching range. From the door, he said, "She's just using you."

"And I thank God for it. I hope she uses me the hell up."

Pierce made a disgusted sound, turned and left. The door clanged after him. Max watched him go, then closed the blinds, flipped the Open sign to Closed and locked the door.

"I don't think he noticed anything about the café, do you?" Lacey asked anxiously. "You can't see much from the diner and he's never been here before, so the Quonset hut wouldn't throw him."

"I think the last thing on his mind was the café, Lacey," Max said, walking toward her with his most seriously sexual look.

Probably the jerk was already on his cell phone squealing to Wade about the cowboy making out with his sister. The irony wasn't lost on Max that he'd managed to stay out of Lacey's bed all this time only to be accused of it because of a crazy scheme she'd cooked up.

"Thanks, Max, for going along with me," Lacey said hesitantly, taking a backward step.

"Going along with you? Why wouldn't I, when it was the truth?" He grabbed her by the waist tight against him. "I had no idea you were serious, Lacey. I thought you just wanted a boy-toy. This changes everything."

"Does it?" Lacey stared up at him, her eyes wide with shock. He fought a grin. He'd have to answer to Wade soon enough, but in the meantime, he'd teach Lacey the danger of playing with fire. He just hoped he could do it without getting singed.

"Oh, yeah." He gave her an I-mean-business kiss, then pulled back, trying not to laugh at the amazement on her face.

"Reeeally?" She snatched that puffy lip between her teeth worriedly and looked like she wanted to bolt.

Well, whaddya know. Here was the answer to the problem of getting Lacey to lose interest in him! All he had to do was call her bluff and she'd head for the hills. Maybe set her sights for a biker instead of a cowboy next time.

"Really," he said, leveling his gaze at her. "Now I see we have a future together."

"We h-h-have?"

"Sure. I'll be taking off in a month and you can come with me. You'll be done here anyway with the café and all. I was thinking of heading up to Oregon, maybe do some logging."

"Logging?"

"Yeah. I'll log and you can keep house in one of the cabins out there. Sometimes the plumbing's a little iffy, but, hell, you've got the great outdoors for your potty. You told me how much you love being outside. And for baths you can heat water over the wood stove—after you gather the wood, of course. As long as you look out for bears and snakes."

"Bears and snakes? Max, we need to think about this. I don't know about me and logging...."

"Maybe you'd like Colorado better," he said to drive home his point. "There's a sheep ranch I know where they'd hire me. Now, sheep are a lot more work than cattle, but maybe you'd get into it. Help with the shearing. Dye the wool, maybe knit me a sweater for the long, cold winters."

"I have a job in Phoenix, Max. I can't move. And I don't even know how to knit."

"Don't you want us to stay together?" He tried to look sad.

"Well, I..." She studied him, her green eyes clouded with worry in her pale-as-flour face. She was chewing the hell out of that bottom lip. He'd love to get in a nibble himself. He felt sorry for her and intensely aroused at the same time. What the hell, maybe just one kiss.

When his lips touched Lacey's, Max felt like he'd touched a live wire. His entire body vibrated with wanting her. Lacey made a little sound of surrender in the back of her throat and their tongues met like long-lost friends. His fingers kneaded her back, then moved up to the back of her head, into those thick curls, until he could feel the skull of that precious head that held her diamond-hard ambitions and ridiculous schemes. He cupped her head and held her close to him.

She trembled against his upper body. Her fingers went into his hair. She pressed herself against him so hard she seemed to want to crawl inside him, and he wanted her to. Oh, how he wanted her to. His hands moved to her blouse. With a quick jerk he untucked it, then slid his fingers under the fabric to press into her soft skin for a second before he went where he wanted to go—under the lace of her bra to caress the breasts that had been taunting him since she smeared coffee grounds across them that first day. He found the front clasp of the bra and flicked it open. The cups flipped away and he had full possession of her breasts, soft and solid and better than he'd imagined.

Lacey was moaning into his mouth, then trying to say something. He had to touch more of her. He needed to get this blasted blouse out of the way to allow full range of motion, then take off his own shirt. Distantly, he knew this was a mistake. He'd been playing with fire to teach her a lesson, but now he could smell something burning. Him. But he didn't care.

He'd released her mouth, and gone for her buttons when Lacey whispered, "Maybe we could work something out."

"Huh?" he mumbled, still dazed.

"Maybe I could visit you in Oregon and you could visit me in Phoenix and—"

"What?" His fingers froze on button number two, as the reality of her words reached him. He looked at Lacey, her eyes cloudy with lust, her mouth kiss-reddened, her skin flushed. She was sex-crazed, pure and simple. He knew the score and he had to take charge.

He did the only thing he could do. He pretended

she'd been joking. "Very funny, Lace," he said. His chuckle sounded choked and dry.

"Huh?" She shook herself, then blinked. The flash of hurt in her eyes made his heart ache. He almost dropped the routine and told her everything—about his promise to Wade, his fake cowboyhood, everything. But that wouldn't help. He stuck to the best thing. "You were just kidding me," he said. "Going along with me like I went along with your Pierce act."

"Oh. Sure," she said with an even worse laugh than his. "Right." She backed away, straightening her blouse, reaching under it to reattach her bra, a partstightening move he tried not to watch.

"You had me going there for a second." He gave her a gentle buddy-slug in the arm. Her face was so translucent, he could see every feeling. He felt like a complete jerk. His only consolation was that pretending it hadn't happened would be the best thing for her.

"Yeah." She laughed and slugged him back, but she looked completely miserable, like a cat in the rain.

"Well, I better get going," he said, moving away, ignoring the way his pants pinched. He hoped she couldn't see his erection. Between the saddle horn and false alarms with Lacey, his parts were getting quite the workout. "See you tomorrow?" he said, backing toward the door.

"See you," she said, but she didn't meet his gaze, and she looked absolutely defeated. He wanted to make love to her just to make her feel better, but he knew that would be a huge mistake. For her, and, suddenly he realized, for him, too.

MAX WENT straight to the phone and called Wade. He got voice mail at the office, where Wade seemed to live. No answer at home, either. Damn. He began to pace. How long would Pierce wait to tell Wade? Maybe he'd pout a day or two. Nah. He looked like a whiner. *Lacey doesn't want me anymore. She's sleeping with a cowboy...boo-hoo-hoo.*

Max couldn't let Wade get the wrong picture, dammit. He'd behaved honorably...more or less. He'd let his libido scream for more and fought it down. He deserved credit for that, despite what that schmuck Pierce would say. Wasn't Wade's cell number somewhere around here? This qualified as an emergency for sure.

"Wade here." The man actually sounded jovial. Max could hear laughter and music in the background. Great, Wade was at a social function. Just the time he wanted to hear that Max had been making out with his sister.

"Max McLane. Sorry to bother you after hours, but—"

"Hey, Max. Glad you called. I looked over the new statement you faxed up. Looked good, except I'm not sure you should have bought that equipment new."

"Those cooling units don't depreciate and with their lowered cost they'll pay for themselves in six months," he said quickly, wanting to get to the point, "but, listen—"

"I think the grand opening costs are a tad high, too."

"It's within range. And it's part of the marketing budget, which we'll balance with reduced advertising the first month." Plus, it would give Lacey more to be proud about, but he wouldn't share that little detail.

"You're the numbers man," Wade said with a light chuckle. "I trust you."

Maybe not, after what he had to say. Max grimaced. "Listen, Wade, I need to talk to you about Lacey."

"She didn't pick up on the dummied budget, did she?"

"No." She thought he was a whiz with numbers. She didn't know Wade had authorized an infusion of capital and, if Max had anything to say about it, she never would.

"Good," Wade continued. "She's getting what she wants, so she should be happy. Is she happy, Max?"

"Happy? About the project? Yes," he answered truthfully. As for the rest, he was afraid to think about it. "Listen, something just happened and I want to explain it to you before Winslow does."

"Winslow? What's Pierce have to do with anything?"

"He was just here at the café."

"Down there?"

"Yes. There was an incident with Lacey."

"An incident?" Wade went instantly tense. "What happened? Did Lacey get hurt?"

"No. She's fine." *More or less.* "Evidently, Lacey had broken up with the guy, but he wouldn't accept it, so she wanted to...um, illustrate her point."

"What did she do?" Now Wade sounded weary, braced for another Lacey stunt.

He took a deep breath and spoke quickly. "She suggested that we—she and I—pretend we were, um, seeing each other."

"Seeing each other? You and Lacey?"

"Yeah. So we did that—" he prayed Wade wouldn't ask him to draw that erotic little picture, "in front of Pierce. I'm sorry, Wade. It was ridiculous, and I should have argued with her, but I just didn't..."

His words faded and Wade was silent. Here it came: *How could you? I trusted you with my sister and you took advantage of her, you lecherous bastard. You destroyed her engagement, ruined her future...*

Then, abruptly, Wade laughed. "And Pierce actually fell for that?"

"Yeah. As a matter of fact, he did." And why not? Max had almost been convinced himself.

"It's just so impossible. You and Lacey, come on."

"Yeah, impossible." He tried to laugh along, but Wade's reaction irked him.

"She thinks you're a cowboy, for God's sake."

"Some women have a thing for cowboys, you know," he said, a little grumpily.

"Oh, right. The 'bad boy' thing. Not Lacey. She's just trying to prove her independence. From me, mostly, but looks like Pierce got lumped into the mess. That's a damn shame. Those two are good together. They'll probably work it out once she's back here."

"I don't know. He struck me as kind of, I don't know," *a weak, weasely jerk* "wrapped up in himself."

"Oh, really? You think so?"

"Just a first impression." *And I could take him.* The primitive reaction bothered him still.

"I'm sorry Lacey dragged you into that," Wade said.

"Not a problem." It wasn't exactly cruel and unusual punishment, he wanted to say. He could still taste her sweet mouth and feel the weight of her breasts in his hands.... *Stop it.* He was supposed to be apologizing for what had just happened, not reveling in it.

"My sister is the most difficult, stubborn girl in the world."

She's not a girl, she's a woman, you idiot, he wanted to say. *From the top of her curly head to the tips of her edible toes. And so sexy that no man in his right mind would turn her down.* Instead, he took a deep breath and said, "So, anyway, I just wanted to tell you what happened, so if Pierce calls you, you don't get the wrong idea."

Again Wade chuckled. "Relax, Max. I know you'd never make a move on my sister. You're my stand-in. Thank God it was you and not some real ranch hand who'd maybe get rough with her when she changed her mind." Wade blew out a breath. "I'm just glad you're there watching out for her."

Great. Now Max really felt like a heel. Wade trusted him so much he'd never believe Max would be cad enough to sleep with Lacey.

He hung up, but instead of feeling relieved that Wade still trusted him, he felt strangely deflated. And a little resentful of an undercurrent he'd picked up in the conversation. Like maybe Wade's trust was based not so much on his faith in Max's honorable intentions, but on his sense that Max wasn't Lacey's type. Type meaning class. That possibility started an anger simmering in him.

An anger fed by the alarming realization that he wanted Lacey. Bad. His desire for her had grown with each moment together to the point where he could barely contain it. It wasn't her ridiculous ploys to trick him into sex. And it wasn't just lust, though that was definitely part of it. It was her. Just her. She'd crashed through every barrier he set up against her with her bubbly energy, her fierce, vulnerable eyes, her determination, her intelligence. He loved the way she nibbled her lip. The way she looked up at him, her every feeling on her face. It had become a moment-by-moment struggle to keep from crushing her to his chest and kissing them both to madness. He certainly couldn't laugh it off like Wade had.

And he loved how kind she was—supporting Ramón, even when he was being ridiculous, hiring his siblings to help the family out and always looking out for Jasper, whose workshop was a hole in the ground where she poured money.

She had such a generous heart. If only she gave herself the kind of support she gave those around her. That's why he was so glad she trusted him, depended on him for his ideas and his business sense. That made him feel good.

And horrible. Because he was a liar and a fraud. Even if it was for her own good.

And if she knew who he was? Max sighed. If she knew he was an out-of-work accountant about to try his hand at construction, her attraction would probably pop like a bubble. Lacey wanted a high-profile corporate life—a life Max had left for good.

Wade was right. They were an unlikely match. So, he should just focus on the job before him. They both should. Lacey's job was to prove herself to her brother with the Wonder Coffeehouse. Max's was to make sure she did it without blowing the budget.

Yep, a relationship with Lacey would be absolutely impossible, no question. And that was exactly what made Max think they just might belong together. Holding that thought, Max headed for Lacey's trailer.

8

WHEN LACEY opened her door to Max, her eyes went wide and her pixie grin flickered, then faded. "What's wrong?" she asked soberly, as if only something terrible would bring him to her.

"We need to talk."

She blew out a breath. "Not you, too. That's what Pierce was always saying."

"Can I come in?"

"Okay," she said, hesitating. "If you think you have to." She backed up to let him in. Her face looked tired and her eyes were watery. He'd put that pain there and it made him ache all over. He'd promised himself never to hurt her.

The small trailer seemed to close around him, making it hard to breathe. Lacey felt the closeness, too, because she backed away from him.

Stubbornly, he stepped closer. "I want to explain about what happened earlier."

"There's nothing to explain. I forced you into a little charade and you turned the tables on me. It was a joke. No biggie." She tried to laugh.

"I didn't mean to hurt your feelings."

"You didn't. And the important thing is you helped me get free of Pierce, once and for all."

"But I didn't mean to sound like I didn't care, because—"

"I know you meant well. Let it go." But her eyes were dark and her voice hollow. "Of course I couldn't go to a sheep ranch or a logging camp with you. You were right to make me see that. Pierce was right, too. I have been playing games, and I got so caught up in trying to get you to bed with me that I've been acting like a teenager. Making a pest of myself." Her voice wobbled.

"Not at all. You are incredibly attractive, Lacey." He gripped her by the shoulders so she looked up into his eyes. "Don't you know how hard it's been not to just grab you? I've had to fight like mad to keep from...you know."

"Don't. Please. Don't pretend." He saw her lip tremble, then she caught it between her teeth in that way that sent a charge through him. "It's ridiculous to get obsessive over something as stupid as sex. I lost focus. I've got to finish this renovation and then move on. My whole future's ahead of me."

She smiled through her tears and he saw how determined she was. And how vulnerable. And he realized he couldn't argue with her. And he couldn't kiss her. She was right. Her future *was* before her. And he couldn't be part of it. She deserved more than that arrogant twit Pierce, but she deserved more than him, too.

He released her arms. "You know, you're a remarkable woman, Lacey Wellington."

"I'm just me," she said, managing a smile.

And that was remarkable enough for any man.

LACEY SHUT the trailer door on Max's retreating form with an uneasy feeling there was something more Max had wanted to say. What was it? He'd seen something in her face that had made him hold back. She pulled open the door, started to call him.

No. What was over was over. The whole point of that little "come logging with me" bit was cold proof of that. Forget it. She shut the door, rested her back against it, and looked at the empty trailer that would never again host a steamy moment between her and her cowboy. Tears dropped onto her folded arms.

Oh, get a grip. She palmed away the tears. The ridiculousness of her plan to sleep with Max suddenly overwhelmed her and she laughed at herself. She'd actually been ready to take a crack at gathering wood in the forest, dodging bears and snakes, just to be with Max. The thought made her hot with embarrassment.

Going to bed with Max had been a stupid goal. Not without its charms, but not worth going to extremes for. If she wanted to have wild sex with a he-man, it would just have to be someone besides Max McLane. For whatever reason, he didn't want to play.

And at least Max had helped her get rid of Pierce. That was the important thing. If a by-product of that was that she'd gotten rid of Max, too, then so be it. All the same, tears kept filling her eyes and spilling over her lids.

Oh, stop it, she told herself. *It was just sex.* Nothing earth-shattering. Except she was pretty sure that with Max it would come close.

THIS WAS IT. The morning of the opening. Two months' work would come to fruition tonight and Lacey's nerves jumped like water on hot oil. Her excitement almost made up for her disappointment about Max. Almost. She'd resigned herself to the decision to stop trying to get him to bed, but it hadn't been easy.

As the pace of the work escalated, they'd worked more closely together. Max was practical, knowledgeable and calm, and running an idea past him always resulted in a better one.

Unfortunately, when she bounced something off him, it always came back with a jolt of desire so intense she could hardly focus on what they were talking about. Every accidental touch was like brushing against a hot stove. She was forever bracing herself against the sensation, trying to hide the way she trembled when he got close and lost all rational thought when he looked at her a certain way.

Once she'd come around a corner too quickly and crashed headlong into him. He'd caught her in his big hands and held on for a long tense moment, his eyes glittering with longing. She'd barely kept herself from lunging upward to kiss him.

She told herself it was just the forbidden fruit phenomenon—the thing denied became the thing most craved—but that didn't help much. Nights were the worst. Sometimes, as she lay sleepless, she imagined dashing across the highway in her nightie to wordlessly pounce on him in the bunkhouse, like some lace-trimmed temptress of the night. Of course she had more sense than that. Barely.

Luckily, working on the coffeehouse kept her hands and mind busy. And tonight everything was coming together. A few last-minute things had to be handled. The new chairs for the cocktail tables hadn't arrived when expected and neither had the cocktail napkins, but she'd been promised on-site delivery of the chairs and overnight shipment of the napkins. Ramón was swearing in Spanish and banging things in the kitchen as he prepared the hors d'oeuvres for tonight. At least Ramón was acting normal.

To calm herself, Lacey surveyed the room. Everything looked just as she'd envisioned it. The stage's wood gleamed, flanked by expensive speakers. The new round faux granite tables looked both elegant and trendy. The walls, painted a rich plum and cranberry, with salmon accents, held some of Jasper's funky art pieces including a rendition of the Grand Canyon made out of wine and champagne corks, Van Gogh's "Starry Night" in bottle caps, and an impressionist self-portrait of Jasper made from shellacked hot dog condiments—ketchup, relish, chopped onions and mustard.

Suspended from the ceiling were kidney-shaped pieces of plywood painted with animal stripes or spots. The zebra-striped bar stools complemented the swaths of fabric in leopard spots and tiger stripes that swagged here and there on the walls. The effect was trendy and retro, colorful and lively. Exactly what she'd had in mind.

The black lacquer on the new bar shimmered and the diner area shone with new paint, fresh accents, a gleaming brass espresso machine and a stunning selection of baked goods. Even the Amazatorium looked better. She'd dusted everything, added new pedestals and had the signs painted in the same typeface as the new neon sign out front. She'd even designed a new costume for Monty Python.

At the grand opening, they would serve special coffee drinks at reduced rates along with a selection of Ramón's pricey hors d'oeuvres. Max had convinced her it was worth the expense to make a splash. Ditto the fabulously expensive band. It worried her a little, but she trusted Max. Thank God for Max. He'd been her rock this last month. Even if he hadn't been her lover. The thought made her ache.

There he stood, a few feet away on the ladder, tacking up the last piece of faux animal skin to the top of the stage. She sighed. He still looked so good. He made a much better employee than a sex object, she told herself. This was a much more sensible way to behave. Every time she was tempted to go for a redo on that last visit to her trailer, she thought about how humiliated she'd felt when she took his joke about sheep shearing seriously.

There was some satisfaction in the fact that he seemed to be suffering, too. Now and then she caught him with a look of raw heat that stopped her heart.

This was better, she kept telling herself. She'd just gotten carried away, fixated on sex with Max as if it were part of the café renovation. Now she had one focus. Much better. More clear, more purposeful.

More lonely. Just looking at Max made her feel empty

inside. But that was how it had to be. You had to make sacrifices for the things that mattered.

Speaking of which... She opened her phone to call Wade to remind him about tonight. Damn. Voice mail again. Ironically, Wade had been so hands-off with her since that first week she'd had trouble getting his attention when it counted. She'd invited him to come at six for an early dinner, when she planned to wow him with a tour and then a PowerPoint computer presentation—complete with bullets and sound effects—about the project.

Now her gaze was drawn to Max, who climbed down from the ladder and backed away, admiring his work.

"You think the staples will hold?" she called to him. The fabric sagged heavily in the middle. "Maybe you should use nails."

"You're the boss," he said, grinning at her, completely nonplussed by her micromanaging.

"I just want to be sure," she said. "I want everything to be perfect for Wade."

"Forget Wade. It'll be perfect for *you*. That's what counts."

"The way I handle this project will show Wade what I can do. Things have to go like clockwork."

"You want the coffeehouse opening to go perfect so you can leave it?"

"Pretty much."

"But you love it here."

"It's great, but this is just one restaurant. Soon I'll have all of the Wellington properties to worry about. This is only short-term." Every time she got Wade on the phone she made sure to ask about the California buyout, so he'd know she was interested in the bigger picture, even while every ounce of her energy felt locked in to what she was doing at the Wonder Coffeehouse.

"Happiness is happiness, short-term or not." Max's dark eyes locked on hers. Whenever he looked at her she felt so *seen*. He had the uncanny ability to read clear through her.

"All the same, I'd feel better if you nailed the swag," she said to distract him from her simmering doubts.

"Okay," Max said, sighing. He started back to the ladder. Watching him walk away she automatically wanted to call him back. She felt better when he was nearby—even if she couldn't really *have* him. It was stupid—some biological response she couldn't control.

"Truck's here with the chairs!" Rodney yelled through the archway. "And a UPS carrier dropped off some boxes."

"Must be the napkins with our logo," she said. Great. The chairs and the napkins. Two things off her last-minute checklist.

"I'll help unload," Max said and headed out. For the next few minutes, the place swirled with movement as Max and Rodney placed the chairs around the café tables, and Jasper carried in boxes and boxes—and boxes—of napkins. She hadn't ordered that many, had she?

She went outside to sign for the chair delivery and see the truck off. She returned to the coffeehouse and noticed something awful. The chairs were only two inches below the table height. No human could sit on one and fit his legs under the table. No wonder they'd been a steal! They were off-size.

At that realization there was a huge thud from the kitchen. *"Madre de Dios!"* Ramón shouted.

Before that catastrophe had a chance to sink in, Jasper said, "Uh-oh," from where he'd opened one of the napkin boxes.

"What?"

Jasper held up one of the cocktail napkins. It showed the silhouette of a well-endowed woman's torso and said The Rack. Great. The napkins were wrong. *Vulgar* and wrong.

Ramón marched through the archway holding the oven door in two mitts. "This fell off!" he said accusingly, as if she'd deliberately sabotaged the thing.

"I'll handle it," Max said, pulling a screwdriver out of his jeans and following Ramón to the kitchen.

The phone rang, so she hurried after them to pick it up in the kitchen. Jasper came with her. This better not be bad news.

Max answered the phone before she got there. "That's too bad," he told the caller. "No, we'll be fine," he said, then hung up, looking perplexed. "The band can't make it."

"No!" she said, ice filling her veins.

"They're stranded in New Mexico. Food poisoning."

"Oh, wow," Jasper said.

"Great," Lacey said. "What else can go wrong?"

A sudden cry from the stage area answered her question.

The four rushed to the archway. The swag of tiger-striped fabric Max hadn't had time to attach more firmly had dropped onto Rodney, toppling, as it fell, the statue of Venus in sugar cubes beside him. The faux-fur-covered Rodney staggered around in the mound of shattered sugar cubes.

At that moment, the lights dimmed, went black and the AC stopped dead. The power was out.

Great. Everything was falling apart around her. Lacey felt panic lock her chest and go for her throat. "What am I going to do?" she whispered to herself. She wanted to burst into tears, but she knew she couldn't.

"You can handle it," Max said softly, near her ear. "You know you can." He leveled his gaze at her in the gray daylight.

And she did know it. She *had* to handle it. Everything had to go perfectly tonight. She took a deep breath and surveyed the scene. "Okay, we just blew a fuse," she said in her most managerial voice. "Ramón, go flip the breaker."

Ramón ran outside and in a few seconds, the AC and lights kicked back on. Whew! One down, bunches to go. Then her eye fell on the circular saw Rodney had used the day before on some moldings. She went to it and picked it up.

Ramón's eyes filled with horror. "Hold on, *chica*. You don't want to hurt anybody." He backed up, holding up his hands.

"Don't be ridiculous," she said, sparing a smile. She plugged in the saw, revved it up and marched over to one of the chairs, which she set upside down on the stage. She buzzed exactly four inches off each wooden leg, flipped the chair back up and slid it smoothly under the table. "Voilá!"

Everyone applauded, so she took a little bow. "Can you handle the rest, Ramón?"

"*No hay problema,* boss."

"Great, because..." She looked at her watch. "I've got to orient the waitresses to the Wonder Coffeehouse customer philosophy."

"How can I help?" Jasper asked. For once, she had his undivided attention.

"Get the list of bands we auditioned and call for backup, would you?"

"You got it," Jasper said and hustled off.

"Rodney, would you fix the oven? It'll need welding." If it weren't an emergency, she'd have liked to do it herself. She liked welding and had actually done a couple of plumbing joints under Rodney's supervision. Rodney set off, so she turned to Max. "Would you nail the swag, please, and maybe clean up the mess?"

"Your wish is my command."

"Thanks. After you're done, would you go into town and snag some generic napkins to hold us over?"

"I'm on it."

Blowing out a breath, Lacey headed for the diner where the new waitresses would gather any moment. So far, so good. Assuming Jasper got a decent band, they'd be back on track. Just a broken brick on the road to the Emerald City. There was no way she'd let tonight go wrong. Everything depended on it.

TWO HOURS LATER, Max returned from his errands. He entered the diner, then moved into the stage area where he stopped to watch Lacey in action. The four waitresses were huddled around her at the computerized cash register behind the liquor bar. They all wore the zebra leotard, skirt and beret Lacey had modeled for him that long-ago day. None of them looked as good in it as she had.

He watched her explain the machine, demonstrate, then let them try it on their own. He wanted to remember her exactly this way—a ball of happy energy—coaxing, checking, fixing, adjusting, making things happen. He wouldn't have many more chances to see her like this. After the opening, he'd have finished his favor to Wade and his supposed handyman job, and he wouldn't have any reason to hang around Lacey.

He would stick it out on the ranch a little longer, though. Riley Stoker was making progress on his business plan and wanted a little more help. Riley had soaked up his advice like a sponge and already had some accounts for his halters. Plus a friend of Riley's was a custom bootmaker who wanted to pay Max for a consultation or two. That would be fun.

Max had also helped Jasper get a small-business loan for his gallery. He'd enjoyed that, too. Interestingly enough, the loan officer had mentioned that the chamber of commerce got lots of requests for small-business start-up advice, which made him wonder about maybe starting a consulting business....

Nah, he'd decided he wanted to work with his hands. He was probably just looking for things to distract him—

self from how much he wanted Lacey. Luckily, the Tucson construction firm could take him anytime, so that would take his mind off all this. Lacey, most of all.

She'd be gone soon anyway, he reminded himself. Back to Phoenix to the stupid corporate job she thought she wanted. She loved it here, he could tell. When she talked about that business baloney, her eyes went dead.

Lacey must have felt his eyes on her, because she looked up at him and her face filled with joy. "Max!" she said, rushing toward him.

His heart skipped at the sight. He was such a sap.

They kept having moments like these when their gazes locked and he couldn't hide how much he wanted her. At least after she left he'd no longer suffer the constant temptation of her nearness. He would be glad of that. Sort of.

"You brought flowers!" she exclaimed, when she reached him.

In his pleasure at watching her, he'd forgotten that he'd bought tiger lilies to put at each table—his contribution to the grand opening.

She took the large bundle, buried her nose in their blossoms, then looked up.

The look on her face—gratitude, pleasure and hope—made him want to yank her into his arms, flowers and all.

"There are so many," she said. "You sweet man. You shouldn't have." She took a step toward him, her eyes full of emotion. Oh, God, she thought they were for her.

To correct her impression, and keep her from hugging him, he said, "They're for the tables," he said. "For color."

"Oh, sure." The light in her eyes faded. She set the bundle on a nearby table, then looked up at him, her face composed. "They'll be perfect. Thanks, Max."

"You've done a great thing here, Lacey," he said to change the subject. "No matter what anybody says."

"What would anybody say?" She looked panicked.

"Nothing. No one will say anything. Everything's great. Don't worry."

"Sure. I'm just nervous, I guess." She was so easily shaken, so uncertain of herself, his heart ached for her.

He longed to hold her, make her feel better with a comforting hug, a touch of her cheek, a gentle kiss....

"I'm going to miss the hell out of you, Lacey," he blurted. He'd meant to *think* the words, not say them.

"Miss me? Where are you going?"

"I'll be...um, moving on soon."

"Oh. That's right," she said glumly. "You're going to Oregon to log. I guess I hadn't thought that far." Her eyes held his.

"You'll be leaving, too, remember?" he said.

"I know. I'll miss you, too, Max." Her eyes searched his face, wanting to know how he felt about that. He fought like hell to hide from those green lasers.

"I'll think of you," he said, knowing he shouldn't say it.

"Me, too."

"A lot." Why couldn't he shut the hell up?

"Me, too."

Acting on impulse, he touched one springy curl of

her hair. "I just regret one thing," he said. *Shut up, shut up, don't say it!* But looking into the depths of her green eyes, touching her hair, he just had to. "That I never...that we never..."

"Had sex?" she finished breathlessly.

The words grated on him. *Made love.* That's what he wanted—to make love to her. But he couldn't say that, so he only nodded.

"Oh, Max," she said, and threw her arms around him. The suddenness of her move caught him off guard. He took a backward step, then another, but couldn't catch his balance and crashed into a plaster pedestal, dislodging the stylized globe it held, which delivered him a glancing blow on the head before bouncing away. Max landed on the floor.

Lacey crouched beside him "Are you all right?" She studied his head where the globe had conked him. "You've got a lump already. I'll get something."

And then she was gone, leaving him with a lump on his head and regret in his chest. He didn't know if he was more sorry about the kiss or the fact there wouldn't be any more. The gods of physical calamity had smiled on him again, though, and kept him from getting carried away with Lacey. This had to be the last time. He might not survive another encounter. As it was, he'd be lucky to live through whatever cure Nurse Lacey de Sade returned with.

Six forty-five and everything was perfect, Lacey thought. Six exotic coffees were brewed and ready. Bottles of various liqueurs gleamed from behind the slick black bar for the coffee drinks. Rows of oversize cobalt-blue mugs awaited coffee orders. Each granite cocktail table sported a tiny black vase and two of the tiger lilies Max had bought. The smell of rich coffee, baked goods and Mexican spice filled the air. Tiny tamales made of white chocolate with pistachio nuts, mini-muffins and brownies in three flavors, and shrimp *flautas* with *chipotle* chile and grilled pork quesadillas—new creations of Ramón's—waited patiently in trays to be passed.

The waitresses giggled nervously and fiddled with each other's berets.

Everything was perfect. Except for one thing. No Wade. Lacey bit her fingernail nervously—a habit she'd given up as a teenager. Wade hadn't shown up at six as he'd promised and hadn't responded to his cell phone. Reluctantly, she'd shut down the PowerPoint presentation and put it in her trailer.

He'd just have to see the place in action first. She hated to admit it, but her success wouldn't be real until she saw that "wow" on Wade's face. What if he didn't come at all? No, he'd said he had details to handle on the California sale. He'd probably be here any minute.

"You look great," Max said from behind her.

She turned to face him. "Thanks." She loved how his eyes lit at the sight of her and the way that slow, sexy, wild-west grin spread on his face. His teeth were so white. He had great hygiene for a ranch hand. "You look great, too."

He did. He looked stunning in a black cowboy hat with a white dress cowboy shirt and string tie, black jeans and shiny black boots. Her cowboy. If only she hadn't pushed him into that globe. That little thump had shattered the moment. Not exactly the way she'd hoped to rock his world. Since then, she hadn't had a chance to talk with him. But, in her heart, she hoped that after the opening they'd pick up where they'd barely started. But what if Max came to his senses? He had a bad habit of that.

Max studied her face. "What's wrong?" he said. He read her too well.

She wasn't about to tell him her immediate worry, so she told him the other one. "Wade's not here yet. I'm scared he'll miss it."

"He won't," he said. "Besides, even if he doesn't come, you're still a success. Enjoy it."

"Sure," she said, but she couldn't really. Not yet. Not until the place was packed with happy customers. And Wade *had* to be here. "I've got to find Jasper. He got a band, but I want the details."

"I think he was checking on Monty," Max said.

She headed in that direction, but the door clanged. Her first guests! Lacey's heart lurched. She took a deep breath and headed out to greet them.

Before she knew it, the place was packed and Lacey was breathless from greeting people and talking about the place with reporters. Her cheeks hurt from smiling so hard. Trying to catch her breath, she looked around at the people who filled the bar stools and all of the cocktail tables, and stood in clusters everywhere else, talking excitedly. There was definitely some picking up going on, too. Perfect.

It was hectic, though. Lots of little fires to put out.

Every time she turned around she had to reassure Ramón that people loved his food. It was worth it to watch him beam.

Luckily, Max was helping wherever he was needed—serving drinks when the waitresses got too busy or keeping the college boys from getting too rowdy, pausing now and then to catch Lacey's eye with a grin. She found herself always aware of where he was. She felt his eyes on her, felt his support, his pride, and it filled her with energy and confidence.

Still no Wade, though. She tried not to be disappointed, but she felt like a bride left at the altar. She wished she'd arranged to have the event videotaped. There would be TV news coverage at least, so she'd have to settle for buying the video news clip to show him.

She looked at her watch. Quarter to eight. The band should have set up by now. Where were they? She'd yet to get the details from Jasper. Panicked, she set off after her uncle. She found him about to go behind the stage curtain. "What's happening?" she hissed.

"Everything's fine," he said, his eyes bright with excitement.

"Is the band ready?"

"Actually, the first two groups I called had gigs, but my friend Art helped me line up something."

"We have no band?"

"Calm down. We've got something just as good. Three acts, as a matter of fact. Don't worry."

"Don't worry? But I—"

"Trust me," he said. He held a finger to his lips in a

"ssh" gesture, then slipped behind the curtain. Lacey wanted to go after him, but the guests seated at the tables were watching, so she turned and smiled as if this were all going according to plan, then moved to the side of the stage. She caught sight of Max at the back of the room, his arms folded, watching her with such pleasure and pride her heart warmed. She just had to hope it would be all right.

The curtain opened and Jasper stepped out to the microphone. "This thing on?" He tapped the mike, the noise like thunder.

Lacey cringed.

"Welcome to the Wonder Coffeehouse, Theater and Amazatorium," he said, blaring like the voice of God until he adjusted the mike's distance from his mouth. "As I was saying. The old Wonder Café and Amazatorium got a face-lift thanks to my niece here." He pointed at where she stood beside the stage. "Didn't she do a great job, folks? Let's give her a hand." He clapped against the mike, each clap a harsh amplified thud.

Obediently, the people clapped and Lacey blushed and nodded, trying to give Jasper the signal to get going.

"Now, before we get started, let me just put a plug in for the Amazatorium. Be sure to stop in. You can say hello to The Thing, and enjoy the wonders of the desert I've collected over thirty-five years. There's a two-headed bobcat, a five-foot-high tumbleweed and—"

"Jasper," she hissed.

"Okay, Lacey. I getcha. Enough already with the

commercial. But, seriously folks, do get yourself a souvenir before you leave. A key-chain, pot holder or pocket mirror." He caught Lacey's frown. "Okay, okay. Let's get started with our first performers. You're in for a treat tonight, because...fresh from an exclusive engagement at the Copper Queen in Bisbee, Arizona—we were lucky to catch them on their way to Quartzite—I present to you..." he paused dramatically and then shouted, "Manny Romero and his Polka Trio!"

Before Lacey could absorb the incongruity of linking the name "Romero" with "polka," three rotund Hispanic men clomped onto the stage wearing lederhosen and leather Tyrolean hats, and accordions hanging from their necks.

The audience seemed stunned. A few people laughed, assuming this was a comedy routine.

But it wasn't. The trio swung into the "Beer Barrel Polka," their brown faces intent, the feathers in their jaunty caps jiggling from the intensity of their movements. They were good, too.

After a few shocked moments, she saw that Max was loping across the dance floor to her. He took her hand and swung her into his arms. "Smile, sweetheart," he said. "And think Lawrence Welk." And then, amazingly, they were dancing. Max led her skillfully through several quick polka turns. The audience began to clap in time. Someone whistled. If she hadn't been so flipped out, she might have enjoyed the way the air brushed her cheek, the polka rhythms made her want to move and what a wonderful dancer Max was. She kept thinking, *Manny Romero?*

"Folks, get out here and dance," Max called to the watching crowd, motioning with one hand. "Hey, Buck," he said, spotting the ranch foreman. "Get your lady out here and cut some rug. The Texas Two-Step works great!"

There was some noise, chairs scraped, and soon Buck and a petite woman began to dance. Lacey recognized her as the waitress who'd served them at the cowboy bar where she'd gotten smashed. "I swear the things you get me into," Buck muttered to Max, a tight smile on his face as they danced by.

"You look good, honey," Buck's partner said to her. "Just stay clear of boilermakers and you'll have a fine time."

Lacey smiled. As more people joined them and the crowd clapped along, she began to feel better. Okay, the guests were going along with it. And at least Manny and his *compadres* were decent musicians, though how they ended up as a polka band was beyond her.

After a few numbers, Manny and the boys waddled off to uproarious applause. All right. They'd squeaked by without sending the crowd home.

"Thank you, thank you, thank you," Jasper said, sounding like a circus barker at the mike. "Just a sample of the kind of entertainment you'll see every night here at the Wonder Coffeehouse, Theater and Amazatorium. Next up, we have a very special act. Making his debut here with us tonight, is a master of prestidigitation, a minister of the mysterious, a wonder of the wand, the one, the only, Kenny the Magnificent."

A boy no older than thirteen lugged a card table onto

the middle of the stage, then threw a tablecloth over it. He wore a crooked moustache, a silk magician's hat that rested on his ears and a cape that hung to his knees.

"Thank you," he said, then bowed stiffly. He performed a couple of simple card tricks, and then announced, "For the rest of my performance, I'll need the help of a lovely assistant." He searched the audience, then his eyes fell on Lacey. "How about you, Miss?"

"Me? Oh, no."

"Sure, go ahead," Max said, giving her a nudge.

She glared at Max, but the audience was cheering, so she hiked up her skirt and climbed onto the stage. Okay, how bad could it be?

Pretty bad, it turned out. Instead of being Kenny's lovely assistant, she became his accidental comedy foil. Trick after trick failed. He cracked an egg on her head from which a bird was supposed to hatch. Instead, the egg broke, dribbling yoke and white down the side of her head and the bird had to be chased across the stage.

The water in the pitcher that he poured into a folded newspaper she held, which was supposed to disappear into thin air, spilled down her blouse. And the scarf he tried to pull out of her ear got tangled in her hair and had to be cut out. His finale, in which he was to magically free her bound feet and hands, required Max and Buck to untie the knots that were cutting off her circulation.

The good news was the audience loved it. They hooted, laughed and cheered uproariously the entire time. Kenny was glum at first, but eventually the crowd's applause cheered him up.

When Kenny had taken his final bow and dragged his card table to stage left, Lacey climbed offstage, her blouse damp, her hair sticky with egg, and focused on the one good thing about the performance—her brother hadn't seen it.

Except then she noticed a man leaning against the wall beside the door, his arms folded, a huge grin on his face. Wade had arrived.

9

OMIGOD. She could only hope he'd just walked in. "Wade!" she said, her heart in her throat.

"Lacey." Wade pulled her into a brotherly bear hug, then released her. "You're damp."

"Yes, I, um," she brushed at the water-soaked blouse. "There was a spill…"

"So I saw."

"You saw?"

"I walked in just as the egg broke on your head."

"The first or second?"

"There was more than one?"

"Oh, God. Let me explain, Wade. You see, the band I'd scheduled got some bad *chorizo* in New Mexico, and Jasper had to—"

"Relax, Lacey. It was fine. The crowd loved it." He indicated the happy, chatting people who still filled the place. No one had left, that was certain. If anything, the coffeehouse was more crowded than ever. "The place looks great."

"You think so?"

"Absolutely."

"I wanted to surprise you," she said. He hadn't even boggled at the transformation. It was almost as if he expected it. A tingle of disappointment edged her pleasure.

"Oh, you did. You really did," he reassured her.

"Good. It was all my idea." That sounded self-important, so she hurried to explain. "I mean, I did the research and planning and everything. My crew made it happen. I have a whole presentation I want to show you. We could do it now, if you'll come with me to the trailer."

"No need, Lacey," he said. "You're busy now. We can go over all of it tomorrow. I'm staying at Rancho Gordo tonight. I'll come out here in the morning and we can talk."

"Tomorrow? We'll talk tomorrow?"

"Yeah. Over breakfast. I understand you've replaced Jasper with someone who knows his way around *huevos rancheros*."

"What time?"

"I don't know. How about nine?"

"Nine it is. Sharp." How could Wade be so casual? He'd been second-guessing her all his life, and just like that, he trusted her judgment? She'd spent thousands of dollars changing the look and purpose of a Wellington property without telling its CEO and he was willing to talk about it over *breakfast*? She was stunned.

"So, tomorrow we'll talk?"

"Sure, sure," he said, then his attention locked on something beyond her shoulder, and his jaw dropped. "Would you look at that...."

She turned toward the stage just as Jasper said, "And now I present to you...Miss Pepper, the Bird Woman of

Mystery!'' A woman in a purple harem outfit emerged from stage left. She clapped her hands and Middle Eastern music filled the room. Pounding drums and wailing reed instruments sounded so good through the new speakers it seemed like a live band was playing. The harem woman began to chink finger cymbals and swung her hips into a belly dance.

A belly dancer? Jasper had outdone himself this time, she thought. She looked back at Wade, expecting him to be laughing. Instead, his gaze was locked on Pepper. He looked absolutely smitten. She'd never seen Wade show a twinkle of interest in any female.

Pepper was pretty, Lacey saw—short, with long brown hair and substantial breasts. Though her technique wasn't great, she danced with exuberance. After a few more circles, she stopped still, put both pinkies to her mouth and gave out an ear-splitting whistle. A few seconds later, a huge white bird—an overweight cockatiel, Lacey thought—appeared on the stage, waddling leisurely toward Pepper and then began to walk up her leg. As soon as the bird reached her arm, Pepper began to sway her hips again in a slow arc.

Looking almost bored, the bird walked up her arm to her shoulder where it tugged at a string that released a veil, which dropped to the stage floor.

The audience howled its delight. Pepper did a little shimmy, then spun around. Eventually, the lumbering bird had plucked five veils, one by one, from Pepper's body. In the end, she wore a bikini that covered everything important—at least enough to keep the state from yanking Lacey's liquor license.

As a finale, Pepper did the splits, while the hulking bird flew across the audience—a battleship with wings—three veils trailing like streamers from its beak.

The crowd cheered, Pepper took a bow and the guest on whose shoulder the bird landed walked it back up to the stage, wobbling a little under the weight of the gargantuan bird.

After the applause ended, Lacey turned to Wade. "The entertainment's a little kooky tonight, but we'll get that ironed out."

But Wade was hardly listening. "We'll talk tomorrow, Lacey," he said. "I've got to meet that woman." He headed toward the stage.

"Okay...tomorrow," she said, still puzzled by her brother's relaxed attitude. It was a *good* thing, she knew, but it felt all wrong.

She looked for Max to tell him what happened and get his opinion about her brother's reaction, and saw he was helping the bartender. But, as usual, he felt her eyes on him and looked up.

She headed for him, tugged as if by a wire, needing to be near him.

He handed off the drink to a waitress without looking, keeping his eyes on her. He came around the bar to meet her halfway. Her heart pounded in her throat so that she could barely speak. There was still so much between them.

He looked like he wanted to hold her, but at the last minute, she saw him get control and stop.

"That was your brother you were talking with," he said. "How did it go?"

"He was pleased. Well, not upset anyway. I don't know quite what to think he thinks. He didn't really seem surprised. I'm meeting him for breakfast at nine to show him my presentation. I'll know more then."

"I'm sure he'll love what you've done," Max said. "How could he not? He probably has more faith in you than you realize."

"Maybe." Though that was hard to believe.

"Are you happy?"

Was she? She'd been so anxious, she hadn't thought about it. "Yes, um, I think so." She should be. Everything was going her way, even if Wade's reaction seemed a little strange.

"Good. I want you to be happy. That's the most important thing." His gaze roved her face, as if memorizing her, his eyes full of longing and sadness.

Embarrassed by his intense look, her hand flew to her egg-bedraggled hair. "I'm such a mess," she said.

"No, you're not," he said, low and serious. "You're beautiful." His eyes held her as if she were a gift just for him. She could hardly breathe for how much she wanted him.

"All night, I've been trying to memorize you," he said. "While I held you in my arms dancing, when you were standing on stage, looking gorgeous and elegant even with raw egg sliding down your cheeks or being hog-tied by that squirt magician. I want to remember every moment of you."

"Why are you telling me this?" she asked, knowing already that he was saying goodbye. Oh, no. She'd wanted to erase his regret about not having sex with her. Tonight would be a perfect chance. "But, Max, I thought we would...I mean...before..."

"I know. But that would have been stupid. Thank God I got conked before I went too far. This worked out for the best." He crushed her into a hug. "Lacey," he whispered in her ear—so much more in the word than just her name.

Before she could say anything, he was gone.

She wanted to go after him, argue with him, at least kiss him goodbye, but duty called. Jasper beckoned to her from the stage—Kenny wanted a letter of recommendation—then the bartender needed more wine and there was something annoying Ramón in the kitchen.

Over the next two hours, while she kept things moving, solved minor crises and made sure her customers were happy, Lacey kept an eye open for Max, but he seemed to be gone. She had the icy feeling he meant for that last hug to be goodbye for good. If she wanted to see him again, she'd have to track him on horseback.

She tried not to think about that, focusing instead on how well everything was going, on what she'd achieved tonight.

Finally, at 1:00 a.m., Lacey left her staff to attend to the stragglers and clean up, and headed for the door to go home. She was almost too exhausted to appreciate the amazing sight of Wade in rapt conversation with Pepper, the well-endowed belly dancer, at a table, while the gargantuan cockatiel pecked peanuts from his hand.

She pushed through the door, anxious to go home, lie down and analyze the evening. She missed Max, wanted to talk about everything with him, but he was probably fast asleep in his bunk. She missed him, but she wouldn't let that ruin her triumph.

She stepped out into the warm night. The stars were tiny and bright in the desert sky and seemed to be shining just on her. She heard an owl hoot and, far away, a coyote howl. Nearby, crickets set up a soothing racket. She was so tired, she could hardly walk.

"Finally."

The relieved voice was Max's. Lacey whirled and saw that he was sitting on the coffeehouse porch. He held a matchbox in one hand and was shaking out a match with the other. At his feet was a large pile of what looked like burnt twigs, but obviously were matches.

"Max! What are you doing here?" she asked. "And what are you doing?"

"Well, it's this way," he said, dropping the match and its box, pushing to his feet and walking slowly toward her. "I meant to leave. I had every intention of leaving, but I just couldn't get the sight of you out of my mind." He reached her and put his arms around her waist, tugging her to him. His eyes gleamed in the moonlight.

"So I made a deal with myself. I had this box of matches, see, and I decided that I would start burning the matches one at a time, and if you didn't come out by the time I'd burned them all, then it was over. I was done and I would go."

"You've been out here burning matches for two hours?"

"Well, I had to get another couple of boxes, but, yeah,

that's what I've been doing. And I was on my last one when you walked out."

"Perfect timing," she said, her heart starting to pound.

"I'll say. I've got a blister the size of a dime on my thumb." He held it up.

"Let me kiss it better," she said and pressed her lips carefully to its tip.

He made a sexy, hissing sound. "Oh, don't stop there," he said. "I think I'm going to need first aid all over."

His words thrilled her, but she looked into his eyes. "What does this mean, Max?"

"I don't know. It's insane, but I just couldn't let you go like that...without...I don't know." His eyes searched her face.

"I'm so glad," she said. "It would have been humiliating to chase you out to that bunkhouse." Tears sprang into her eyes.

His hands cupped her face, so warm, so strong, so Max. "There's not much point, Lace. I know we have no future together. We're different people going different directions."

"But we can have tonight, can't we?" she said. "Just tonight?"

"You think we can manage that?" he asked sadly. "Really?"

"We have to at least try."

There was both surrender and command in the way he kissed her. It was such a relief. She didn't have to lunge at him or flirt with him or ask him point-blank.

He just kissed her. Long and slow and sweet and full of the promise of more to come.

When she was so light-headed, her vision was black at the edges, Max released her mouth and said the words she'd longed to hear since she'd watched him eating Jasper's pie. "Let's go to bed."

"Finally," she said, feeling the delicious thrill of it.

He held her tight against him as they headed for her trailer. She felt so good tucked under his arm, breathing him in, aware of each finger pressed into her flesh.

When she'd walked out of the coffeehouse, she'd been so exhausted she could barely walk, but now, realizing what would happen once they reached her trailer, adrenaline rushed through her in waves, and she'd never felt more awake. The crickets thrummed a steady pulse that served as counterpoint to her erratic one.

They reached her door, and she turned to him, suddenly shy and a little nervous. She began to babble as she felt for her key. "I think it went well tonight, don't you?"

"It went great, Lacey," Max said softly, his voice low, intimate.

"The hors d'oeuvres were a big hit. And they loved the mint-chocolate-chip coffee. That was a great idea."

"Absolutely."

"I heard a reporter interviewing a customer, who went on and on about the, quote, hidden mystery of the Amazatorium. If they like the Amazatorium, they'll like anything."

"For sure."

"And people want Manny Romero back." She found her key and pulled it out. She caught the way Max was looking at her, his dark eyes glittering and hungry, and thoughts of the opening flew from her mind.

"You did great, Lacey," Max said, his arms around her. "You should be proud of yourself."

"I am. I really am." Not only had she gotten her coffeehouse, but she was about to get her cowboy, too. She couldn't believe it.

Except Max didn't seem like a cowboy anymore. Looking up at him, tall and handsome in the moonlight, she saw just Max. The man who'd helped her, supported her, who'd waltzed her across the floor at the opening night of her coffeehouse. The man who'd brought her lilies, crunched her numbers, hammered the stage together crookedly and hung the curtains too loose. The man who was now going to take her to bed.

Under the cowboy hat, which now seemed like just an article of clothing, Max's eyes were full of feeling. There was need, all right. Plenty of that. But there was also affection, caring...maybe even something stronger? She wasn't sure and was afraid to even imagine it was possible. This *had* to be just sex, as she'd promised him all along.

At last she was getting what she wanted from Max. And she didn't need to get drunk or try to seduce him or anything. All she had to do was this. She stepped up on her tiptoes, put her hands on the back of his neck, lifted her face and met him halfway.

Instantly, a flash fire of desire burned through what remained of her nervousness and she wanted Max more than anything else in the world. More than the coffeehouse, more than her career, more than her brother's respect. All she wanted was Max. Just Max. Something about that was dangerous, she knew, but right then, under the stars, in the dense summer dark, she didn't care one bit.

AS THEY STOOD at the door to Lacey's trailer, the air thick with their desire, Max felt filled up by Lacey. She'd soaked into his skin, smothered his senses, permeated his brain. The way she felt in his arms shut out everything—his promise to Wade, his false identity, his secret job and his imminent departure from the café, the Rockin' W...and her life.

Once inside the trailer, he made himself hold back, take his time, except she kept kissing him with that incredible mouth—searching with her tongue, moaning into his mouth, wanting him as much as he wanted her. He wanted in. She wanted him in. Now.

Her blouse had come untucked, so he reached under it, sliding up, pushing her bra out of the way to cup her breasts, while their tongues moved and slid and pushed for positions that went ever deeper, more suggestive— promising what their bodies would soon do. She tugged at his shirt and the snaps gave way. Great idea. Ditch the clothes. He released her long enough to let her rip his shirt open. He let it drop off his arms to the floor.

Her eyes widened at the sight of his bare chest and she made a sound that turned into his name. That made him surge. If he wasn't careful he'd climax before he even got her to a horizontal surface.

He yanked her to him, kissing her again, one hand holding her tightly to him, the other cupping the tender flesh of her breasts, then stroking the tight knots that were her nipples. She felt so good. He wanted more of her. All of her. He'd waited two months for this, wanted it, fought it, and now he was going to have it. He didn't care about Wade or his promise or whether or not there was any future to this. He just wanted Lacey and he'd see what happened after that.

Abruptly, Lacey pulled away to fumble with the buttons on her blouse. She gave up and yanked the blouse over her head and tossed it to the floor, sending her bra immediately after it.

The sight of Lacey bared for him—just him—made Max's insides go weak. The moonlight shining through the curtains of the darkened trailer gleamed white on her pale skin, her breasts high and firm, rising and falling with her harsh breaths. Her eyes glittered with lust and her hair seemed to glow in the unearthly light.

For me, he thought, *she looks this way for me*. The idea filled him with a primitive possessiveness that made him want to grab her to him and say, *you're mine*.

"You are so beautiful," he said instead, and he cupped her face in his hands. "And I want to make you mine." She quivered and her breath came in rapid pants. She seemed to have trouble catching her breath.

"I—I'm...so...glad that we're...I'm just..." She kept trying to suck in air. "I'm so excited I feel numb. I...can't...breathe. I'm afraid I won't be any good."

"It's okay," he said and pulled her into his arms, managing a chuckle through the pounding of his lust.

His chest swelled with emotion, with the desire to protect her, with the overwhelming sense of how precious she was.

Something had changed in him, he realized. Something big. The reason he hadn't slept with her before was because it would mean more to her than it would to him. Now he realized it might be the other way around.

That was okay, he decided, loving the way she felt in his arms, the way he could feel her heart beat, hear each precious breath. He'd just have to handle it. To be with her like this was worth every bit of misery afterward. And maybe, just maybe, she felt the same as he did.

He nuzzled her neck and whispered to her. "I'm as excited as you, Lace. In fact, if you look at me one more time like that I just might embarrass myself right here in your living room."

"Really?" she asked so eagerly he smiled against her neck. Her breathing slowed a little.

"Oh, yeah." He pulled back to look at her. "Don't you know how hot you are? How you turn me on?"

She didn't answer, just looked at him wonderingly.

"I guess I'm going to have to show you." He swung her into his arms. "Every way I can think of. All night long."

"Oh." Her fingers locked around his neck. "You have the best ideas." She rested her sweet cheek on his chest.

"And like they say, if at first we don't succeed, we'll just have to try, try...and *try* again."

She shivered at his words, gratifying him. He carried her down the narrow hall, careful not to bang her plump little toes against the wall.

BY THE TIME Max had carried her to her bedroom door, Lacey had managed to slow her breathing to as normal a rate as she could expect considering she was about to make love—um, have sex—with the man of her dreams. She'd been hyperventilating like mad. It would have been humiliating to faint on him, but she couldn't bring herself to ask him to fetch her a paper bag to breathe into. At least her vision wasn't gray anymore.

For a second, she wished he wasn't a cowboy, a no-mad who'd be heading off to a sheep ranch or a logging camp or who knows where. She wished he'd be some-where close by, so she could see him all the time. That didn't make sense, of course. His whole appeal was that he wasn't the kind of guy she could see every day. He was wild and free and he'd stay that way. She could see it in his eyes—the passion there could never be civi-lized.

No, she had to do what she'd promised him—accept this as the fling she'd told him she wanted from the be-ginning. That had to be enough. So far it was more than she'd dreamed it could be. Max was carrying her into her bedroom in his arms like Rhett Butler in the movie. It was so sexy, so romantic, so perfect....

Then he tripped on something—probably the cowgirl boots she'd left on the floor—and they both crashed onto the bed, which promptly broke. Again.

They slid down the tilted mattress, laughing, until Lacey's back reached the wall. Then they looked into each other's eyes and desire burned away the laughter. Max's lips met hers and his fingers caressed one of her breasts. She went liquid with lust.

She pushed herself against his erection, wanting more and more. Reading her mind, his hands slid under her hiked-up skirt and his fingers slipped beneath her panties and found her. She went electric. Heat and ache rushed through her. She wanted to touch him, too, to see him, so she pushed her hand inside his jeans.

He groaned and broke off the kiss. "Easy there. You've got me so hot I don't think I can hold out."

"So, don't," she said.

"But I want to be inside you," he said. "I want you around me." And the way he said it made her want it, too. She withdrew her hand. Max reached into his jeans pocket and produced a condom. "The coffeehouse bathroom is well equipped," he said.

"Customer service," she breathed.

Then Max's fingers started doing incredible things to her, and the banter died on her lips. His mouth found one breast and sucked, then nipped it, drawing her desire like a thread that stretched tautly from her sex to her breasts.

She moaned and writhed, powerless before this pleasure and ache.

She was in his hands—literally—and she gave herself up to the sensations. The tension built, the thread stretched, taut and more taut, until she knew she was at the brink of climax.

"Oh, oh, oh. I'm going to—"

"Wait for me," Max murmured and gently withdrew his fingers. He pushed off his jeans and underwear, and as magically as a movie dissolve, the condom was on and Max was on top of her. He gently pushed her legs apart, and she opened them even further, wanting him inside her now.

And then he was there. Easing in. She could tell he was using all his concentration to keep from slamming into her. *I did this,* she told herself with a thrill. *I made him this hot.* She loved the chivalry that seemed to come so naturally to him.

She moaned, loving the feel of him there, hard, yet giving. He eased in farther and farther. She reached to hold his muscular behind, to push him, urge him on, loving the movement of taut muscle she felt there with each of his thrusts inside her. This was for her. All for her. And then he was in all the way, and he began to move in and out. She moved with him, lifting her hips for more—more pleasure, more of him, giving him more of herself.

He seemed to know exactly what she wanted and when. As if he were in her mind, as if her pleasure were his pleasure, as if he were under her skin.

"Lacey," he moaned. "Lacey." He said it like a prayer and she answered it with his name. And then, with the next thrust, she felt her release come in a wave. A wave that went on and on.

Again she cried his name, surrendering to the spasms. She felt him climax within her, intensifying her own pleasure.

Afterward, they held each other for a long silent moment. Max was so big he felt heavy on her—like the best blanket of all. She smelled his delicious smell, felt his warm breath on her neck. Their legs were intertwined, their bodies wet with shared sweat, their hearts pounding in muffled counterpoint. Their breathing was ragged. She felt so good with him holding her, so right. As if the two of them understood everything about each other and about sex. She never wanted this to end.

Lying there, panting, feeling Max's lips on her neck, she realized something even more terrible. Max was right. This wasn't *just* sex.

Maybe it could have been if they'd done it that first night after the almost-brawl in the bar. But not now. Now she felt connected to him in more than a physical way. She knew him so well, and he knew her—saw inside her, understood her.

She thought of all they'd shared, how close they'd been as he'd helped her achieve her dream. He'd become part of her dream. And now she wanted him to be part of her life. This was more than sex. This was love. She was in love with Max.

Lacey opened her mouth, needing to say something, but Max lifted his face to her. His expression told her he was thinking about lust, not love. "So, what do you think?" he asked wickedly. "Was it good?"

"Was it good?" It was heaven on earth.

But before she could form the words, with a phony frown, his eyes gleaming with lascivious intent, he said, "Hmm, you're right. I guess we'll have to try, try again." And then his fingers found her, slick and wet for him. "You'll let me know, won't you? When I get it right?"

The instant hot charge of his fingers on her sent her agonizing discovery to the back of her mind, and she gave herself over to Max and the pleasure of his touch. And to hours of try, try, trying again.

MAX'S EYES flew open, except something blocked one eye. He brushed at the thing, then realized it was fingers. Lacey's fingers. She was stretched alongside him, half on his body. He was in Lacey's bed, he knew, so why did it feel even harder than the bunkhouse cot?

Because he was lying against a wall. He remembered that the bed had broken. They'd obviously succumbed to gravity in their sleep. Not very comfortable, but worth every neck crick to have Lacey lying on him like this. He looked past her soft curves and riot of hair to squint at her bedside clock. Six o'clock in the morning.

They'd only been asleep for two hours. They'd crammed a lot of lovemaking into the previous three. His body ached all over, but that wasn't the worst pain he felt.

He'd fallen in love with Lacey. Something he shouldn't have done. Something she didn't want. Or at least that's what she'd said.

Gently, so as not to waken her, he brushed her curls out of her eyes, so he could see her face, the way her fair eyelashes were soft half circles on her cheeks—so sweet, so innocent, her mouth soft in sleep. She looked like an angel.

But she'd made love like a demon, he remembered, getting aroused at the thought. She'd been a responsive lover who gave and received with such intensity she'd simultaneously worn him out and made him beg for more.

Now he was in love with her. He wanted to wake up with her every morning. That meant things had to change. He'd have to tell her who he was—a frustrated accountant hired to watch over her. A poser. She wouldn't like that. Not one bit.

But surely, she had feelings for him, too. He thought of her sex-flushed face, her cries of passion. No one could make love the way she had without feeling more than lust. He had to hope that her feelings were strong enough to withstand the truth about the little deception he and Wade had cooked up on her behalf.

Maybe he could convince her to stay here instead of going back to Phoenix. She was happy here at the café. He could work construction in Tucson. She could move into his house.

Yeah. Maybe this could work.

What if it didn't? He couldn't help asking himself. What if deep down Lacey was like Heather? What if, when push came to shove, she did want a rich, ambitious paper-pusher like Pierce Winslow? No, there was more to her than that. He'd seen the joy on her face when she worked on the café. She liked real work, too, just as he did. Work that engaged her body and soul, not just her intellect. And if she loved him like he loved her, everything would fall into place from there.

Nervous about the next step, Max had to get up. He didn't want to wake Lacey. She needed her sleep. The restaurant opening had exhausted her and he'd done his best to finish her off. With a last, loving look at her sleeping form, he carefully climbed out of bed, grabbed his abandoned clothes and tiptoed out of the room.

10

THE FIRST THING Lacey noticed when she woke up was that her body ached all over. But it was a satisfied ache, like from a good workout. In a quick rush, she remembered exactly what that workout had consisted of. Sex with Max. Instantly, she wanted round two. More like round six. She'd lost count.

But Max was not in the bed with her. She noticed how bright the light was and checked her clock. Eight-thirty. She'd slept in. Then she saw a note on Max's pillow.

Didn't want to disturb you. Went to take care of a few things. I'll meet you at the diner for lunch and we can talk...about everything.

He wanted to talk. That gave her a shiver of pleasure. That was so uncowboy-like. Maybe she was wishfully thinking, but even cowboys settled down eventually, didn't they?

No, she was still in the afterglow of all that lovin'. Max might have feelings for her, but would he change his whole life to be with her? Unlikely. He'd bristled when she'd suggested going into bookkeeping. And she sure couldn't trail him around the west from cabin to campground to ranch. Even though, the way she felt right now, she was ready to buy a tent. That was the haze of infatuation. When that cooled down, she'd be back to her real life. And real life centered on her breakfast meeting with Wade.

Wade! She'd almost forgotten. He was meeting her at nine at the diner. Nine sharp, she'd said, so she couldn't be late. They'd be planning her future, hopefully, setting the date for her to join the corporate team.

She scrambled into the shower, but even as she tried to think about what she'd say to her brother, she couldn't get Max out of her mind. She clung to the shreds of what they'd shared the night before. As she washed herself, she remembered how he'd felt inside her. And his touch on each body part. His mouth had been there and there and *there.* She even had a bite mark on her ankle. Ooh. He'd spent a lot of time on her toes. She'd never thought of toes as erogenous zones, but, boy, were they.

No, no, no. She had to get her priorities straight. First Wade, *then* Max.

At a quarter to nine she headed for the diner. Wade's red Porsche coupe was already parked in front. Before she walked onto the porch, she paused to admire the coffeehouse. It looked happy and sparkling in its new paint, with its new neon sign of a steaming purple coffee mug set at a jaunty angle. It looked as proud as she felt.

"I did that," she said out loud. "I made that happen." She was so happy. And she loved the place, she realized, so much. *Don't get too attached,* an inside voice warned. She'd have to move on. Still, she felt rooted to the flagstone sidewalk and connected to the quaint building before her.

But her brother wasn't inside. Sandy, the waitress on duty, told her he'd arrived early and Jasper had invited him over to check out his studio. She decided to go over there to make sure Wade saw the possibilities of Jasper's gallery. They'd already gotten bids on the modest construction needed to make the studio into a gallery and Max had helped Jasper get the small-business loan he needed.

Besides, she wanted to get down to business with Wade right away. She had a rendezvous with Max at lunchtime. Lacey laughed at herself. What was the matter with her? She was about to discuss her entire future, but she could hardly wait to hightail it back to her trailer for more cowboy sex. It was like rushing through the prime rib dinner just to get to the chocolate soufflé. But what a soufflé!

As she passed Jasper's trailer, she heard Wade's voice coming from his back porch. She headed in that direction, then heard another voice. A familiar voice that made her stop short. Max. Wade was talking to Max, of all people. They'd never even met as far as she knew. She got close enough to see them, though their backs were to her.

Instinctively, she quieted her steps and walked closer, her ears tuned to their words.

"I mean it, Max," Wade said. "Knowing you were supervising took the worry off me completely. I knew Lace couldn't get in over her head with you keeping an eye on her."

Keeping an eye on her? What? Max had been supervising her? The words echoed in Lacey's mind, the meaning thundering through her like a train through a tunnel. Wade knew Max. Wade had asked Max to watch over her. Her stomach dropped to her toes and her head began to pound. She froze, horrified and stunned, wanting to run, but she had to hear the rest of the terrible story.

"The grand opening was a little pricey."

"She wanted to impress you."

"I know." Wade sighed indulgently. "But at least she's gotten proving herself out of the way. Now I can get her up to Phoenix and she'll settle down. Maybe even give Pierce another chance."

Lacey's blood throbbed through her. They were talking about her like she was a child they'd been indulging.

Wade reached over and patted Max's shoulder. "All thanks to you, Max."

"Don't thank me, Wade. I—"

"No, *don't* thank him," Lacey said sharply, walking toward them on numb legs. "Don't thank him for anything."

Their heads whipped around at the same time.

"Lacey!" they both said. Max jumped up.

"Sorry to eavesdrop, but you *were* talking about *me*," she said bitterly.

"Let me explain, Lacey," Max said.

"No need to. Let's see if I got it. Wade hired you to supervise his airhead sister. Keep me out of trouble."

"It wasn't like that, Lacey," Wade said. "I didn't *hire* him. I just asked him to do me a favor."

"Oh, I'm so glad to hear this didn't cost you any money, Wade. You didn't even think enough of me to let me handle things." Her voice shook and she swallowed down the urge to cry. She turned to Max. "You knew how much this meant, and you let me go along thinking I was doing it on my own." She stopped because she knew she'd cry any minute and she had to stay mad.

"Don't blame Max, Lacey," Wade said. "It was my idea. And, anyway, he was the one who talked me into letting you renovate the place. If it hadn't been for Max, I'd have stopped you the first week."

"You'd have stopped me?"

"It sounded like a crazy idea to me, but Max said your concept was good and you'd done your homework, so I let it go."

"You trusted Max," she said flatly, tears stinging her eyes. "Over me."

"Not *over* you. And, of course I trusted him. He's the head accountant in our Tucson office."

"You're an accountant?" She looked at Max in amazement. Then she thought about those ultra-sharp pencils and how quickly he'd taken to her spreadsheet. "Of course you are. I should have known. 'I'm just good with math,' my Aunt Fanny!"

"I'm not an accountant anymore," Max said.

"Oh, right. I forgot. You're a cowboy. Except you keep falling off your horse. I can't believe I trusted you. I—" She broke off, afraid she'd cry.

"Lacey," Max said. "Please."

"Max was just looking out for you," Wade said.

She whirled on her brother. "This was Max's project, wasn't it? I was just the idiot dancing around thinking she was in charge." Hurt replaced her shock and anger and now she knew she would cry. She turned away to hide her tears.

"It's not as bad as you're making it out to be," Wade said.

"I don't know how it could be any worse. I've gotta go." She half ran toward her trailer.

She heard Max tell Wade he'd go after her, like she was a hysterical female they had to soothe into passivity.

She reached her trailer, just as Max caught up.

"Let me explain."

She opened the door, went inside and tried to shut him out, but he pushed his way in. She backed away from him, steeling herself against him.

"Let me tell you how this happened," he said. He stepped closer.

"Get out! Why should I believe anything you tell me? You've been lying to me from the minute we met!" Tears welled in her eyes and spilled down her cheeks.

"I'm not leaving until you listen to me," he said steadily.

"All right. Whatever it takes to get you to leave me alone." She folded her arms against him, breathing hard, fighting back more tears, trying to stay furious. Fury was strong. Hurt was weak. She wouldn't even sit down.

Talking fast, his hands making quick gestures, Max explained his friendship with Wade, the job Wade got him, his quitting, Wade's ranch job and the favor he'd promised. He stepped toward her again. "Once I saw what a good idea you had, I thought you deserved a chance, so I talked Wade into helping."

She backed deliberately away until the backs of her knees hit her sofa, stopping her. "I didn't need any favors."

"Yes, you did, actually. You were undercapitalized, but what Wade kicked in made up the difference." He smiled sympathetically.

That made her even more angry. "So I didn't even finance it on my own?" She stared at him, her anger growing by the minute.

"Not quite. Almost. Look, this was still your project."

"In name only." She wrapped her arms around herself, in a hug she hoped could hold in her despair.

"All I did was help you," Max insisted, going to her, gripping her by her upper arms. "And it worked out all right. The coffeehouse is a success. You got what you wanted."

"Hardly." She twisted away from him. Against her will, a fat tear dropped onto her cheek. She palmed it away.

"Listen, there's something else important we have to talk about," Max said, his dark eyes earnest and intent, as if the terrible discovery had been only a blip on the screen compared with what he was about to say. He was so darned sure of himself.

"What's more important than this? This was my dream."

"What's more important is the fact that I..." He hesitated. She could see he wanted to reach for her, but her resistance made him keep his hands at his sides. Good decision. If he'd touched her, she might have punched him.

"That you what?" she demanded.

He licked his lips, locked her gaze and said in a rush, "I love you, Lacey."

"You what?" Her arms unlocked and dropped to her sides in amazement.

"I love you. And I hope you feel the same." He searched her face. His was full of longing and worry. "I want us to be together."

"You love me?" Her voice quavered. Max loved her. That was exactly what she'd longed to hear. She'd been afraid it was impossible, but now he was saying it and she felt numb to the words. Everything she'd built had become dust in her mind. So what if he loved her? She felt like the blood had drained from her body.

"I'm sorry I lied to you. I was just trying to protect you." *Forgive me*, said his eyes. He took a chance and gripped her shoulders. She felt desperation in his strong fingers, as he pulled her toward him. He was going to kiss her. As if that would make everything right.

She stiffened, pushed out of his grip and stepped back, afraid a kiss would make her forget the terrible truth.

"Come on, Lacey." He shoved his fingers through his hair impatiently, turned away, then back. "It's not so terrible, is it? You succeeded. You renovated the restaurant, you impressed your brother."

"No, *you* impressed my brother." She stuck a finger at him. "He gave you the credit. I was just the little worker bee, your cute little assistant." She let her eyes blaze at him. "Like Kenny the Magician. And once again I have egg on my face."

"Wade's a little overprotective. Brothers are like that. I am not your brother."

"No, you're not. But you're no different. If you loved me, you should have told me the truth, even let me fall on my face if I had to. At least it would have been my failure. Now I'm right where I started with Wade. I haven't proven anything."

"Who cares what Wade thinks?" Max said. His eyes sparked angrily and he made an impatient sound. "Make yourself happy, not your brother. You made the coffeehouse what it is. Be proud of that. Stay here and manage it. You don't need a corporate job. Hell, you don't even want that. That's not you."

"Don't tell me what's me and what isn't me! You don't understand a thing about me if you could say that." Anger rushed through her. He *was* like Wade— thinking he knew what she needed better than she did. She felt smothered. "I liked you a hell of a lot better when I thought you were a cowboy. A cowboy—even a lame one—is better than a lying, patronizing, arro- gant...*accountant!*"

"Lacey, I love you. I want us to find a way to be to- gether." But he didn't move toward her, didn't try to draw her back. There was angry impatience in his tone.

"How can you love me? You don't know a thing

about me. And I certainly don't know a thing about you, Max McLane. Is that even your real name?"

"Of course it is. Look, if you'd just get off your high horse a minute and be reasonable—see what's happened for what it is—it will be all right. We were a team, okay? Admittedly, you weren't in on the whole picture, but I helped you succeed. And I did it for you, because I care about you."

"You did it for my brother."

"That's bull and you know it. Forget what Wade thinks, forget that corporate crap and stay here where you're happy."

"You can quit and run away if you want, Max, but don't think you can drag me with you. Just because you couldn't hack it in the business world, don't assume I can't."

"I quit because I didn't want that life, not because I couldn't hack it." There was a warning sound in his voice.

"Sure. Whatever. I don't know what to believe about you, Max. Why should I believe anything you tell me? I don't even know if you really love me. I feel like I should demand a polygraph test or something." That was going too far, but she couldn't help it. Her dream had crashed around her feet and Max was telling her she didn't want it in the first place. Who was he, anyway? He wasn't the man she'd fallen in love with, that was certain.

"I'm telling you the truth," he said harshly.

She had to end this. She'd fallen in love with a man who didn't respect her dream or her, a man who'd baby her just like her brother did. "Well, I don't believe you. And I never will. Ever."

"What are you afraid of?" His words were quiet, final sounding, as if he'd figured out something and he was just waiting for her to confirm it.

"I'm not afraid of anything. I just don't want to be lied to. You don't love me. You want me maybe, and you feel guilty for lying to me, but it's not love."

"You don't want to believe me, do you?" he said coldly, but his eyes were hurt. "Because if you believed me you'd have to do something about us. And you don't want to do that. I don't fit into the little corporate suit you've hung up in your mental closet for someone like Pierce Winslow. I'm not him and I never will be."

"At least Pierce Winslow doesn't pretend to be something he's not."

He gave her a long look. "I love you, Lacey. I'm sorry that scares you, but I can't do this by myself. I swore when I found a woman I wanted to spend my life with she'd have to accept me for who I am—and accept herself, too. I may be at a crossroads in my life, but at least I know what I'm looking for. You don't have a clue what you want, Lacey. And I can't help you see it."

"Good. Because the last thing I want is any more help from you, Max McLane." she said, lifting her wobbly chin in defiance. "You and your so-called help can go to hell!"

"Do you mean that, Lacey? Really?" His look was long, serious, demanding. This was for all the marbles, he was telling her. No going back.

"With all my heart." It was the first time she'd ever lied to him.

11

THREE WEEKS LATER, Lacey tapped her Palm Pilot stylus on the marble surface of the Wellington corporate office conference table, and tried to focus on the financial statement the strategic planning team was discussing. Instead, she found herself wondering whether Ramón had fixed the leak in the soda dispenser and whether Monty had molted and how Max looked these days....

Stop it. Be in the now. But the now was gray and dull. Her gaze bounced from the gray marble table to the gray suits of the five men who were in the meeting with her to the gray of the sky out the window on Central Avenue.

She'd gotten what she wanted, after all. Once her hurt had faded enough so she could speak to Wade, she'd shown him her presentation, and he'd pronounced it top-notch and offered her the spot on the management team. He'd done it out of guilt, she was certain, and she hated that. It felt like cheating.

She'd swallowed her pride and taken the job, though, promising to prove herself worthy of the post, even if she hadn't gotten it honestly.

So, she had what she wanted, but the joy of it was thin and distant, more intellectual than visceral. She told herself she was just going through an adjustment period, or maybe she was afraid of success like the self-help book she'd bought: *Your Own Worst Enemy*.

"Lacey, you with us?" Wade called to her from the head of the table.

"Yes, um, sure, what?"

"From your experience renovating the café, would you say ten percent is realistic?"

Ten percent? Ten percent *of* what *for* what? She wracked her brain to remember what the devil they were discussing. "Um, ten percent sounds about right. Sure, ten percent."

Wade rolled his eyes. "Look it over and give me your analysis by Friday, okay?"

"You got it," she said, glancing guiltily around the table. But no one looked at her with disdain. No one treated her like she was the weak link in the management chain. In fact, Wade had several times used the Wonder Coffeehouse renovation as an example of savvy marketing and trend watching, deferring to her on cost projections and demographics. He didn't *act* like he'd given her the job, and he certainly expected her to pull her own weight. She'd just have to find a way to get into it more. She tried pinching herself, but that just made her eyes water. She couldn't stop thinking about Max.

Tricking her with Max was something Wade *should* feel guilty about. If he hadn't dragged Max onto the scene, she'd never have fallen in love with him or gotten her heart broken. She'd be happily figuring cost projections and lovingly digging into strategic planning right now.

But without Max she would have failed with the coffeehouse. That was the worst of it. Wade had counted on Max, not her. Despite her best efforts she'd been babied again.

Pierce caught her eye with a sympathetic smile from across the table. They'd become friends in the past few weeks. He'd begun dating the woman who took the marketing job Wade had intended for Lacey. She was perfect for him. They even had the same personal trainer.

She and Pierce had gone to Alberto's for a Flaming Flan Fantastique for old time's sake, and he'd sheepishly admitted Lacey had been right that their relationship had been held together by habit and inertia. She'd told him she was happy for him, and he'd sympathized about the breakup with Max. Bless his heart, he'd even offered to talk to Max for her. That had been the last thing she needed. Though thinking of the way those two had squared off in the diner did make her smile.

She smiled back at Pierce in thanks.

The meeting concluded and Lacey headed back to her spectacular office with its sleek furnishings and fabulous city view to mope.

She missed the coffeehouse, too, and everything about it. She missed Jasper, Ramón, even Monty Python and that damned two-headed bobcat. The clock on her computer said nine-thirty. Maybe she'd call about that leak in the soda machine. Stuart Paulsen, the temporary manager, would be in by now. Since Lacey hadn't been able to find someone with the right combination of vision, people skills and dedication to take over for her, Wade had asked Stuart, who managed Quixote Con Queso, a successful Wellington restaurant in Tucson, to fill in for a few weeks. Just until Lacey had collected a new set of candidates and found just the right person.

"Hi, Stu," she said when he answered the phone.

"Lacey. Oh. What is it?" He sounded irritated. Was she being a pest?

"Just wanted to know if you got the leak in the soda machine fixed," she said cheerily, "or if you need the number of the repair guy."

"The soda machine's fine, Lacey. I told you before you had everything perfectly organized for me. The restaurant's fine. The weather's fine. Everything's fine."

"Oh. Well, then." She knew that was true, and Stuart had told Wade as much, too. She'd done a good job with the coffeehouse, according to everyone. That took some of the sting out of the way things turned out, but not all of it.

Stuart sighed wearily. "You want to talk to Ramón?"

"If he's not in the middle of something."

"Hang on."

She had to cut herself off—stop calling. Still, her heart began to beat harder as Ramón answered the phone.

"*Bueno.* Lacey, *qué pasa?*"

"*Nada mucho,*" she said. "How's it going with you?"

"*Bien, bien.*" Then there was a pause. "Same as yesterday," he said, knowing what she wanted to know. "He had coffee around eight. Didn't eat anything. Then he went over to help Jasper with his books. He got a new pair of boots. Very fly. From the bootmaker he's working with. Got them in trade."

"Really? New boots?" She knew this was childish—to grill Ramón for details about Max like a teen girl with a secret crush. "Does he seem okay? I mean...is he...?"

"Over you? No. *Chica*, he's got it bad for you. He's all grumpy, man. He's getting skinny, too. You should never have left his ass."

"Thanks, Ramón." Why this ritual exchange made her feel better, she didn't know. Ramón had no way to know if Max was over her or not. He just wanted to reassure her.

The truth was, she still loved Max. The fact had grown larger inside her since they'd parted, ballooning like one of those rafts in a sitcom where someone pulls the string in a closet, filling her to bursting, until she could barely breathe.

She kept telling herself she'd fallen in love with a fantasy cowboy, not the pointy-penciled accountant who was the real Max McLane. But it didn't help. Even though he'd lied to her, dismissed her dream, didn't respect her, wanted to run her life, she loved him. Even though he'd been a *sheep* in *wolf's* clothing every minute they'd known each other, she loved him.

Somehow, it made her feel better to know she wasn't alone in her misery. Luckily, Ramón didn't question this strange dance of grief and regret.

"I gotta go, *chica*. A batch of chiles need peeling."

"Sure, sure. Thanks, Ramón."

"You should come down and check it out around here," he said. "You made this place tick."

"It wasn't just me."

"Without you...*nada*."

Maybe Ramón was right. It had been *her* concept, *her* plan. But it had also been Max's management and Wade's extra capital. "*Hasta luego*, Ramón."

Unsatisfied, but determined to do the right thing, Lacey turned back to her computer, willing herself to get fired up about the financial statement she was to analyze. Her eye caught on the photo she'd taped to her monitor. Max had taken the shot of Lacey, Ramón and Jasper the afternoon of the opening. She held the circular saw in one hand and she was laughing. She'd been so happy. She and Max were just hours away from the most fabulous sex she'd ever had in her life. In this picture, she was filled with hope and anticipation and passion and pride. But it had all been a fantasy—her renovating the café her sleeping with a cowboy and Max falling in love with her.

Enough of that. She had to get serious about her new life. This was her future. This was what she'd wanted. What she *still* wanted. Locking her jaw with determination, she shoved the photo in a drawer, flipped open the folder and got to work.

"YOU'RE GOING tomorrow night, aren't you?" In his usual abrupt way, Wade had stuck his head into Lacey's office without knocking to ask her the question.

"Going where?" she asked, knowing full well what he meant.

"To Jasper's gallery opening, you goof."

"I don't know, Wade. I'm pretty busy here." She *was* busy, working to transform a deli she'd convinced Wade would make a great coffeehouse. But that wasn't why she didn't want to go. She was afraid to see Max again. Especially now that she'd finally gotten into the swing of things here.

"Lacey." Wade frowned and came to half-sit on her desk. "This is Jasper's opening. You can't miss it. It's your place. Don't you want to see how things are going?"

"It's not my place, Wade. You know that." The idea still stung that Max had been in charge of the project.

"Not that same argument, Lace. The Wonder Coffeehouse is pure you. What are you working so hard on, anyway?"

"I'm negotiating equipment purchases right now."

He looked over her shoulder a moment. "Ah, you can do that with your eyes closed."

Possibly true. But she was grateful for the day-to-day tasks and the hands-on work at the deli, since it kept her distracted from missing Max, and reminded her of the Wonder Coffeehouse.

"Nice job on negotiating the lease for the expansion space," Wade said. "I couldn't have done better myself."

"Thanks." She studied her brother. Was this another guilt-laced compliment? She was too weary to wonder anymore. She was a little disappointed that even now that she'd settled in she still didn't have the energy and excitement she'd expected. She'd probably been unrealistic about how it would feel to have her dream come true.

"So, have you figured out who my spy is?"

"Very funny." He was referring to the fact that for a while she'd been suspicious he'd assigned someone to secretly supervise her on the deli project, like he had with the Wonder Coffeehouse. As far as she could tell, he'd given her free rein, budget and all, with no more than the normal reports he required of any project manager.

"You just don't see it, do you?" He shook his head. "I guess I should be glad. If you knew what you were worth I'd have to pay you more." She wished he wouldn't flatter her like that.

"Well, I better get back to it," she said, wanting him to leave. She felt Wade's eyes on her, but she didn't look up. Then he blew out a breath and stood. She heard him walk to the door. Good, he was giving up on her going to the gallery. She just couldn't face Max right now. She'd visit Jasper later.

She looked up to tell him goodbye and found him staring at her.

"Lacey, go to the opening. I mean it." She'd never seen him look so serious. "Jasper needs you there. Other, um, people need you there."

"I don't know, Wade. It's complicated…"

"I'm only your brother. It's your life, like you're always telling me, but I think you owe this to yourself."

"It's too hard right now."

"Sometimes you've gotta suck it up and do it." He smiled, then returned to his normal brusque tone. "Besides, you need to kick some butt at the coffeehouse. Stu's blowing it with the staff. He's no Lacey Wellington."

"I'll think about it," she said, her heart already beginning to pound. For the first time in years, she thought Wade might actually be right.

12

ALL THE WAY to the gallery, Lacey's stomach clutched and her palms sweated. She'd decided Wade was right. She should face things—face Max. And she owed it to Jasper to support him. She was excited to see the gallery, it was true, and anxious to see the coffeehouse again. It was just seeing Max that made her nervous. Though she secretly couldn't wait to see him.

She knew he'd be at the opening. He'd been helping Jasper with the business side of the gallery. Though he'd been a half-assed cowboy and a lame handyman, Max knew his way around a spreadsheet. According to Jasper he had several clients he was helping. He'd set up some kind of consulting service. That was good. More up his alley than construction work, that was certain.

She arrived a half hour after the open house had begun and the Wonder Coffeehouse parking lot was jammed with cars. Clusters of people stood outside the gallery entrance, and she could see the coffeehouse was crowded, too. Her heart swelled with pride. She'd helped make this happen.

She saw with delight that the Quonset hut had been transformed from a temporary-looking warehouse to a happening place. Its corrugated surface had been painted to look like a blue sky filled with fluffy clouds and whimsical renditions of some of Jasper's sculptures. Against the pink and purple sunset, the place looked like something designed by Disney—fantastical and sweet.

The lush dusk held a soft breeze that lifted Lacey's hair the way her heart lifted just being here. It was like stepping out of a smoke-filled bar to cool mountain air. Like stripping off panty hose after a broiling walk across a mall parking lot. Like crawling through a cave and coming out to a wide sky. Like coming home.

That was it. It felt like home. She wanted to hug the place—the gallery, the coffeehouse, even the Amazatorium—put it all in a huge sack and carry it with her. She had the terrible thought that Max might have been right. Maybe she did belong here. She'd been happy here. Really happy. Even hard at work on the deli, she didn't feel anything close to this feeling in Phoenix. The sight wavered before her eyes and she realized her eyes were filled with tears.

No, no. She'd made her decision. She'd live with it. Blinking away the tears, she headed for the gallery entrance, eager to congratulate Jasper and braced for her first sight of Max. What would she say to him?

Inside, country club types in flashy cocktail clothes mingled with young hipsters in funky costumes and brightly colored hair. Everyone sipped champagne from plastic flutes and the place hummed with cheerful conversation. Manny Romero and his lederhosen-clad trio were playing in the back.

The gallery looked great. Huge skylights made the

place feel open and airy. The studio area was separated by a lighted glass barrier. Among the newer sculptures, she spotted familiar pieces that Jasper had spiffed up. The totem of appliances was taller and burnished brightly. The farm implement couple had been placed in a frame of barn-red wood. Art hung overhead, suspended on wire—a giant milk carton with ears and an udder, a barber pole transformed into a rocket. The effect was of bright metal, whimsical shapes and colors, fun and fantasy.

Then she spotted Jasper. He wore worker overalls, with a red-white-and-blue bandana tied over his head in gangster style. He looked like he did every day, except the overalls were clean and he'd let his gray hair flow freely down his back instead of tying it in a ponytail. When he caught sight of Lacey, he called her name and strode toward her.

"Uncle Jasper," she said, hugging him when he reached her.

"I'm so happy you made it."

"The place looks fabulous. How's it going?"

"Great. I've already sold three pieces, and when I wouldn't sell the Eiffel Tower, an architect commissioned me to make another one. He has some downtown renovations he wants me to consider building pieces for. Unbelievable."

"That's great."

"I'm actually going to make some money, looks like. Hard to believe." He shook his head like someone who'd just won the lottery.

"Don't sound so surprised. You're a wonderful artist. Why shouldn't you make money?"

"It's all kind of surreal," he said. "Anyway, did you see it?"

"See what?"

At her quizzical look, he took her arm. "Come here." He led her to the reception desk, beside which stood a five-foot sculpture of stylized wings emerging from strips of steel twisted like flames. An overhead spot created flashing prisms around the sculpture, which was entitled "Lacey's Phoenix." Underneath the title, it said "Dedicated to Lacey Wellington, who made my dream real."

"Jasper," she said, tears springing to her eyes. "I can't believe you did that...I mean, you shouldn't give me that much credit. You did all this, not me." She gestured at the amazing art, the buzzing crowd.

"You gave me the courage. You bought the hut. You suggested the gallery. You were always there for me. You believed in me, Lacey. I wouldn't be here without you."

"But all I did was help you. The project was yours. I—" She stopped as her words echoed in her ears. *All I did was help you.* That was exactly what Max had said about his work on the café. But she hadn't believed him. She'd insisted, like Jasper was doing right now, that he was the one who'd succeeded, not her. But Jasper was clearly wrong.

Had she been wrong, too?

She thought about what Wade had said about her work on the new coffeehouse and how he had asked her advice over the past two months, told her to help Stu with the staff. Maybe he hadn't been complimenting her out of guilt. Maybe he'd meant it. *You just don't get it, do you?* Maybe she did deserve more credit than she'd allowed herself.

She looked into Jasper's kind eyes, moist with emotion. "I'm honored and humbled, Uncle Jasper." She hugged his bony shoulders, then stepped back.

"Now, go find Max and put him out of his misery," Jasper said.

"What?"

"He's a good man, Lacey, and he's been mopin' around here like a bad boy at Christmas."

She didn't even try to act like she didn't care. Her mind was already racing with new thoughts, new possibilities. She had to talk to Max about what he'd done for her and why.

"He went that way. Turn left at the totem pole." Jasper pointed toward the back of the gallery.

Lacey searched the huge room with her eyes, past a Plexiglas bathtub filled with blue water and rubber duckies and a trio of green-haired twenty-somethings sipping champagne. Then she saw him, standing between the giant ice-cream cone and the Eiffel Tower made of barbed wire. In her eyes, he seemed to glow in soft-focus.

She ran to him as best she could through the milling crowd, weaving and dodging until she stood before him, breathless and nervous.

He looked thinner than when she'd last seen him. And sadder. He was wearing a Hawaiian shirt and khakis…and no cowboy hat. This was the real Max McLane, the former accountant, not the cowboy. She was happy to notice that didn't change how she felt about him one bit.

"Lacey." Max's eyes lit at the sight of her, then they seemed to tug at her, full of longing and lust, like he wanted to cherish her and undress her all at once.

"Max." She felt hot all over, and more alive than she'd ever felt in her life. She wanted to fly into his arms, but she fought the impulse. They had to talk first. "Tell me again why you took over the coffeehouse renovation. I think I'm ready to listen."

"Why I what?" His eyes searched her face, puzzled but hopeful. "Okay. Well, Wade asked me to do him a favor, and—"

"Not that part. The part about wanting to help me."

"Oh. Yeah. Sure. My job was to help—get extra funding and watch the budget and—"

"But it was my idea and my work, right? No matter what Wade or you did?"

"Of course. The Wonder Coffeehouse is your creation. Your success. Nothing Wade and I did changed that."

For the first time, she heard him. Really heard him. Without feeling insecure or defensive or betrayed. "And it doesn't matter what Wade thinks or you think about what I did," she said slowly, tears filling her eyes. "It only matters what I think about what I did. All this time I've been fighting to earn Wade's respect, when all along the respect I needed was my own."

Max smiled, soft and slow, and nodded. "Exactly."

His eyes held her, warm and full of love. "You know, you always had my respect, Lacey."

"Really? You weren't just humoring me?"

"Humoring you? Are you crazy? You're amazing. You're smart and determined and good with people. You turned this place around on a dime and still helped Jasper with his gallery. Look at how you found work for Ramón and his family. Lacey, you're a wonder." His face was filled with such love and pride, she wondered how she ever could have thought he would tell her how to run her life.

She'd been blind. Too hurt and insecure to see the truth until Jasper opened her eyes. Her heart brimmed with love for Max and regret over her own stupidity. "I'm sorry I didn't believe you, Max."

"I'm sorry I lied to you, Lacey."

"And you were right," she said. "I do belong here. I don't really want that corporate thing. I realized it the minute I pulled up. It was like coming home."

"You were kind of right about me, too," Max said. "I wasn't running from my old life, but I *was* ignoring my strengths. Construction was not my thing."

"No kidding," she said.

"No need to rub it in."

"Sorry."

"Anyway, I found something else. I've started a little consulting business. To help small companies get off the ground."

"Jasper said you were doing something like that."

"I use my accounting background, but it still feels

real. I've got six clients already through word of mouth."

"That's wonderful, Max."

"I feel good about it."

He looked happy, too. And she had a stab of selfish regret. Maybe he didn't need her anymore. "I'm glad you're happy, then. I guess everything worked out for the best."

"Not quite," Max said and his eyes got that look— that sexy, I-want-you look. "There's one more thing I need to be happy."

She didn't have to ask what it was because he yanked her into his arms and kissed her hard, like he had the night they'd made love. Like she was already his and would be forever. And if she had any say about it, she would. Because he was hers, too.

The kiss—like seeing the café—was like going home, warm and promising and safe. And so lusty she felt like she was about to melt and dribble all down his Hawaiian shirt and comfortable pants, which were getting a little tight around the groin area, she could feel.

Max broke off the kiss and looked at her. "There. Now do you believe I love you?"

She was so woozy she could hardly stand, so she could only mutter, "Do I believe...?"

"Well, let me be perfectly clear then." He kissed her again, even more passionately.

"Okay, I believe you," she gasped afterward.

"Good," he said, brushing his brow in feigned relief. "Because the next thing, I'd have to strip you naked and make love to you right here in front of all these people."

She looked where he indicated and found a grinning semicircle of friends—Jasper and Ramón, Buck, the cowboy bar waitress, and her brother Wade, with, amazingly enough, Pepper, the harem woman, dressed in a purple cocktail dress, on his arm.

Everyone smiled at them. "Looks like you're about to do me another favor, Max," Wade said, her brother's grin broader than she'd ever seen it.

"What's that?"

"Make my sister happy."

"That's not a favor, Wade. That's an honor." He looked down at Lacey, his eyes filled with tenderness. "That's something I want to spend the rest of my life doing. Will you let me, Lacey?"

"If you'll let me do the same for you," she answered.

"Absolutely." Then Max's face took on a mischievous look. "Actually, Lacey, it's a good think you're coming back. There's another building project you'll want to handle. We've got the Wonder Coffeehouse, Theater, Gallery and Amazatorium, but we need one more thing."

"What now?" Wade said.

Max looked lovingly down at her. "A wedding chapel."

"A wedding chapel?" Wade said. "Oh, hell."

"Oh, Max," Lacey cried, looking up into his dark eyes and wise-ass grin, her heart brimming with joy. All she'd hoped about true love—that it meant intense passion, deep intimacy and melding with a soul mate— turned out to be true. And she'd found it all right here. She couldn't believe her good fortune.

"And I know just who the first clients will be," Max finished. He kissed her, soft and slow. Her entire soul rose to meet him. The people around her faded away and she was aware of only him and the way he cared for her. He broke off the kiss. "Lacey, will you marry me?"

She looked into his eyes, seeing not a cowboy, or an accountant, or a handyman, but Max, the man who loved her, supported her and respected her, the man she loved with all her heart.

"Yes, Max. I will...on one condition." She gave him her own mischievous look.

"What's that?"

"That you wear a cowboy hat for the ceremony."

"A cowboy hat?"

"Yes. I can't help it. It's that cowboy thing."

"How can I say no? It's that Lacey thing."

And then they kissed, to the gentle applause of their friends. Neither noticed they'd jarred the foam ice-cream cone. When it tipped over and thumped against them, they were so absorbed in each other they hardly felt the blow. What was one little thump after they'd been hit over the head by love?

This Mother's Day Give Your Mom A Royal Treat

Win a fabulous one-week vacation in Puerto Rico for you and your mother at the luxurious Inter-Continental San Juan Resort & Casino. The prize includes round trip airfare for two, breakfast daily and a mother and daughter day of beauty at the beachfront hotel's spa.

INTER·CONTINENTAL
San Juan
RESORT & CASINO

Here's all you have to do:

Tell us in 100 words or less how your mother helped with the romance in your life. It may be a story about your engagement, wedding or those boyfriends when you were a teenager or any other romantic advice from your mother. The entry will be judged based on its originality, emotionally compelling nature and sincerity. See official rules on following page.

Send your entry to:

Mother's Day Contest

In Canada	**In U.S.A.**
P.O. Box 637	P.O. Box 9076
Fort Erie, Ontario	3010 Walden Ave.
L2A 5X3	Buffalo, NY
	14269-9076

Or enter online at www.eHarlequin.com

PRROY

HARLEQUIN MOTHER'S DAY CONTEST 2216
OFFICIAL RULES
NO PURCHASE NECESSARY TO ENTER

wo ways to enter:

• **Via The Internet:** Log on to the Harlequin romance website (www.eHarlequin.com) anytime beginning 12:01 a.m. E.S.T., January 1, 2002 through 11:59 p.m. E.S.T., April 1, 2002 and follow the directions displayed on-line to enter your name, address (including zip code), e-mail address and in 100 words or fewer, describe how your mother helped with the romance in your life.

• **Via Mail:** Handprint (or type) on an 8 1/2" x 11" plain piece of paper, your name, address (including zip code) and e-mail address (if you have one), and in 100 words or fewer, describe how your mother helped with the romance in your life. Mail your entry via first-class mail to: Harlequin Mother's Day Contest 2216, (in the U.S.) P.O. Box 9076, Buffalo, NY 14269-9076; (in Canada) P.O. Box 637, Fort Erie, Ontario, Canada L2A 5X3.

For eligibility, entries must be submitted either through a completed Internet transmission or postmarked no later than 11:59 p.m. E.S.T., April 1, 2002 (mail-in entries must be received by April 9, 2002). Limit one entry per person, household address and e-mail address. On-line and/or mailed entries received from persons residing in geographic areas in which entry is not permissible will be disqualified.

Entries will be judged by a panel of judges, consisting of members of the Harlequin editorial, marketing and public relations staff using the following criteria:
  • Originality - 50%
  • Emotional Appeal - 25%
  • Sincerity - 25%

In the event of a tie, duplicate prizes will be awarded. Decisions of the judges are final.

Prize: A 6-night/7-day stay for two at the Inter-Continental San Juan Resort & Casino, including round-trip coach air transportation from gateway airport nearest winner's home (approximate retail value: $4,000). Prize includes breakfast daily and a mother and daughter day of beauty at the beachfront hotel's spa. Prize consists of only those items listed as part of the prize. Prize is valued in U.S. currency.

All entries become the property of Torstar Corp. and will not be returned. No responsibility is assumed for lost, late, illegible, incomplete, inaccurate, non-delivered or misdirected mail or misdirected e-mail, for technical, hardware or software failures of any kind, lost or unavailable network connections, or failed, incomplete, garbled or delayed computer transmission or any human error which may occur in the receipt or processing of the entries in this Contest.

Contest open only to residents of the U.S. (except Colorado) and Canada, who are 18 years of age or older and is void wherever prohibited by law; all applicable laws and regulations apply. Any litigation within the Province of Quebec respecting the conduct or organization of a publicity contest may be submitted to the Régie des alcools, des courses et des jeux for a ruling. Any litigation respecting the awarding of a prize may be submitted to the Régie des alcools, des courses et des jeux only for the purpose of helping the parties reach a settlement. Employees and immediate family members of Torstar Corp. and D.L. Blair, Inc., their affiliates, subsidiaries and all other agencies, entities and persons connected with the use, marketing or conduct of this Contest are not eligible to enter. Taxes on prize are the sole responsibility of winner. Acceptance of any prize offered constitutes permission to use winner's name, photograph or other likeness for the purposes of advertising, trade and promotion on behalf of Torstar Corp., its affiliates and subsidiaries without further compensation to the winner, unless prohibited by law.

Winner will be determined no later than April 15, 2002 and be notified by mail. Winner will be required to sign and return an Affidavit of Eligibility form within 15 days after winner notification. Non-compliance within that time period may result in disqualification and an alternate winner may be selected. Winner of trip must execute a Release of Liability prior to ticketing and must possess required travel documents (e.g. Passport, photo ID) where applicable. Travel must be completed within 12 months of selection and is subject to traveling companion completing and returning a Release of Liability prior to travel; and hotel and flight accommodations availability. Certain restrictions and blackout dates may apply. No substitution of prize permitted by winner. Torstar Corp. and D.L. Blair, Inc., their parents, affiliates, and subsidiaries are not responsible for errors in printing or electronic presentation of Contest, or entries. In the event of printing or other errors which may result in unintended prize values or duplication of prizes, all affected entries shall be null and void. If for any reason the Internet portion of the Contest is not capable of running as planned, including infection by computer virus, bugs, tampering, unauthorized intervention, fraud, technical failures, or any other causes beyond the control of Torstar Corp. which corrupt or affect the administration, secrecy, fairness, integrity or proper conduct of the Contest, Torstar Corp. reserves the right, at its sole discretion, to disqualify any individual who tampers with the entry process and to cancel, terminate, modify or suspend the Contest or the Internet portion thereof. In the event the Internet portion must be terminated a notice will be posted on the website and all entries received prior to termination will be judged in accordance with these rules. In the event of a dispute regarding an on-line entry, the entry will be deemed submitted by the authorized holder of the e-mail account submitted at the time of entry. Authorized account holder is defined as the natural person who is assigned to an e-mail address by an Internet access provider, on-line service provider or other organization that is responsible for arranging e-mail address for the domain associated with the submitted e-mail address. Torstar Corp. and/or D.L. Blair Inc. assumes no responsibility for any computer injury or damage related to or resulting from accessing and/or downloading any sweepstakes material. Rules are subject to any requirements/limitations imposed by the FCC. Purchase or acceptance of a product offer does not improve your chances of winning.

For winner's name (available after May 1, 2002), send a self-addressed, stamped envelope to: Harlequin Mother's Day Contest Winners 2216, P.O. Box 4200 Blair, NE 68009-4200 or you may access the www.eHarlequin.com Web site through June 3, 2002.

Contest sponsored by Torstar Corp., P.O. Box 9042, Buffalo, NY 14269-9042.

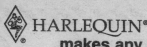